THE HONOR
SYSTEM

THE HONOR SYSTEM

SYSTEM

DICK DABNEY

HARPER & ROW, PUBLISHERS

New York, Hagerstown, San Francisco, London

FIRST EDITION

Designed by Janice Willcocks Stern

Library of Congress Cataloging in Publication Data

Dabney, Dick.
  The honor system.

   I. Title.
PZ4.D115Ho [PS3554.A2]   813'.5'4   75–25078
ISBN 0–06–010951–3

76 77 78 79 10 9 8 7 6 5 4 3 2 1

This book is for

Paul Lawson

One never says a quarter of what one knows.
Otherwise, all would collapse. How little one says,
and they are already screaming.

—*Albert Camus*
Notebooks

1

Her father was all right, she supposed, except that he hadn't any honor. Oh, mundane honor, maybe; telling the truth, what he knew of it, dealing squarely, all that. But it was unimaginative, hillbilly honor, she thought, and she needed somebody to look after her now who had the real thing. Which nobody in Rappahannock, Virginia, did. Or so she believed. Rappahannock was the village she came from, a tiny place tucked up next to the Blue Ridge Mountains. The river was narrow there, not much more than a creek, but they'd named the town for it anyway. Mosby had once jumped it on his horse, a couple of miles from her home. That was Colonel John Singleton Mosby, the Gray Ghost of the Confederacy, a man of genuine honor, to Phoebe London's way of thinking. And she was sure there were more like him, still living.

So she'd climbed aboard the Trailways bus, suitcase in hand, and gone down to Charlottesville, where she hoped and expected to meet honor in a form more tangible than any memory; some young man at the University of Virginia who was Mosby and the poet Lord Byron rolled into one. It seemed the realistic thing to do.

Phoebe London, that pretty blackhaired, violet-eyed girl, gorgeous girl, was not enrolled at the university, though. No women were in those days. She went to a secretarial school about a mile down Main Street from the grounds of the university. The secretarial school was located over a barbershop. Sometimes on her lunch hour she would walk to the Rotunda and stroll about the Lawn. When her lunch hour was over she would come back to the secretarial school, where she was taking courses in shorthand and typing.

It was different from what she was used to. Just the year before, she'd been a freshman at Barnard College in New York City. She'd been making good grades, too, and might still be there if it hadn't been for the nervous breakdown. Her father had ridden up in an ambulance to fetch her home.

For a year and a half after that, Phoebe had been back in Rappahannock, supposedly getting sane. The town's physician, Dr. Codd, had told her that the nervous breakdown was nothing serious, and her father told her that under no circumstances would she be allowed to go back to Barnard. Which was all right with Phoebe. She was determined not to even visit New York City any more, let alone live there. But she didn't want to stay in Rappahannock, either, (pop. 250) where they'd never heard of Lord Byron, and had forgotten about Mosby; where it was rare to see a pair of trousers not mud-besmattered about the cuffs; and where conversation ran to crops and the Depression and local politics.

The chief political issue that summer, for instance, had been between the rich people who hunted foxes on horseback, and everybody else. The foxes were rabid, due

2

to the drought, and the farmers wanted the state to come in and kill them. But the rich wanted them kept alive, for sporting purposes. The rich won, as usual, arguing the case on the basis of their constitutional rights.

Well, Phoebe wasn't interested in politics, crops, or the Depression. None of those things had anything to do with reality, she believed. So she went to Charlottesville, confident that she would meet her young man at the university and that he would sense in her that same quality he had in himself. She did not think that life would be worth living without that.

She had a notion that believing in honor tended to make women beautiful immediately, and men rich in time. She thought the world worked like that. Thus, to her way of thinking, girls who were obliged to be cooped up all day, as she had been, typing under a bare electric light bulb in a windowless room, were paying a kind of penalty for not loving honor enough. Not that she minded work. But she was anxious to get out where the young man could see her. After that she would type for him all his life, if he wanted, or scrub floors. But she had to meet him first, and disliked work without hope.

This was in October of 1931. The term at the university had begun several weeks before, and when Phoebe came outdoors at last, this fall afternoon, she found Main Street thronged with handsome young men in expensive sports jackets, shining white shirts, and regimental neckties striped in orange and black. It was exhilarating to be free, young, and beautiful in this old town, and she was so excited by it that she failed to pay attention to where she was going. Thus she crossed one of those invisible boundaries that she might have wished to stay on the other side of. And suddenly knew from the moonshine reek and whiskey vomit, and from the radio hillbilly music

3

dripping viscously down from a broken window, that she was where she had no business being, coming up fast on a clot of bindle stiffs who were tossing pennies at a crack in the sidewalk.

She kept on walking, of course. She was not going to be intimidated by poor white trash. Having always lived up to her name, which came from Phoebe Ackwards, who had been the fiancée of the illustrious John Witherspoon Cabell, and on whose bony lap she had first been shown the tinted daguerreotype of Cabell himself, who was chief of all Rappahannock legends, coequal with Mosby. Cabell, whose very being, she believed, was grown into the marrow of the gigantic oak tree that stood at the center of Rappahannock and dominated the village. The Yankees had hanged him from that tree after Cabell volunteered himself as a hostage for a man who had nine children. That was John Witherspoon Cabell, a man of total honor, whose pocket watch was Phoebe London's most cherished talisman.

She carried it now, that watch, which had been kept, not as a souvenir, but as a living, indestructible heart, always close about her person, and in her handbag now as she walked down Main Street toward where a husky young bindle stiff was detaching himself from the others, moving to block her way.

This watch, this moving magic, which had been demanded repeatedly of her father by the Daughters of the Confederacy, and which the old man had steadfastly kept; which he had denied to Pastor Lovinhott, who wanted to put it in the tourist museum in the vestibule of the Methodist church; denied it even to his older son, Bill, who wanted to give it to his society wife for a wedding present; and to Peter, the younger son, who wanted it as a gift for

4

a boyfriend; denied it even, finally, to Belle, Phoebe's mother, who wanted it not for itself, but who craved rather the power to withhold it from or bestow it upon any of the supplicants she pleased. The old man, her father, giving it finally to Phoebe herself when he brought her home. To Phoebe, who had not asked for it, but who wanted it most of all, as something that could be depended upon; the Cabell watch being to her not a means of enhancing life, but very nearly life itself, that which beat out red blood into the arteries of her being and enlivened that within herself which she believed to be of an especial honorableness and of an especial affinity for honor in others.

So she had gotten it from her father. Who had gotten it from his uncle, Old Crazy Bob, not as a talisman of any special importance, but as pay, in lieu of cash, in the 1903 panic, when the boy Jim London had to be paid for a year's apprenticeship. Old Crazy Bob, who suggested to Jim at the time that he melt down the gold and sell that. And Old Crazy Bob had gotten it from Cabell himself the day the Yankees hanged him from the ropescarred large limb of the oak tree that stood at the center of Rappahannock. Ropescarred from children swinging. With everyone in the town present at the hanging by order of the Yankee major and everyone looking, too, except Phoebe Ackwards, Cabell's fiancée, who was turned away with the calash top hooded around her and only a swath of black taffeta visible to the doomed man. That Phoebe, the one this one had been named for.

Proceeding down Main Street now Phoebe London was, fresh-looking as new rain on a slick leaf, and with that old watch out of which all her dream life, which is to say all her life, proceeded ticking away now in her purse. And

5

the young grime-faced bindle stiff barring her way. She tried to squeeze between him and the wall, but he wouldn't let her pass.

"How'd you like to lend some money to an educated man?" he said.

She smelled the strong stink of his armpits and saw in her mind now the rows of gray metal filing cabinets at the secretarial school. He reminded her of those. Somewhere close off to her right she heard billiard balls clicking.

Jack Cabell was shooting pool there at the time, at the front window table. He was better dressed than the other hoodlums in the place, although he was a hoodlum himself, a tough, who had grown up in the alleys and pool halls and whorehouses of Charlottesville, and this in spite of having come from a better section of town, over on Second Street. At least it was better than Bottom Wallow, where Aycock's pool hall was. But Jack was as poor as any of Aycock's customers.

He had been coming here ever since the second grade, when the manager had let him hang around in return for emptying out the cuspidors. When he'd gotten bigger he'd stopped doing that. Then he'd had to fight to stay. And had done so, fought on the sidewalk out front or in the pool hall itself. He'd been a desperate boy. It was almost as if he had no other place to go.

Twenty-four now, he had been coming to Aycock's for a decade and a half. Of course, he went other places, too, when he was not working. Although he worked most of the time. Occasionally when he was drunk he liked to hang out at the Negro pool hall up on Vinegar Hill, the one with no name. That was next to the big whorehouse, Marguerita's, where he worked on the weekends as floor manager.

6

He had started going to Marguerita's when he was twelve, to shine shoes. He'd needed the money because his family was poor. Or at least the Cabell part of it was poor. The Cabells, even then, were being supported, some said, not by Jack's father, but by his mother's father. Jack himself didn't know. All he knew was that he felt more at home at Aycock's and Marguerita's than he did at the big house on Second Street, where things were unsure.

And he was tough. By the time his classmates from Central High School began dropping by Aycock's, Jack had been there for almost a decade and was a deadly fighter, quick with his brine-hardened fists, expert in the sucker punch, the knee to the groin, the bottle suddenly broken in confrontation with four or five grown men, or a whole roomful; and he would use the bottle, too. George Gordon, the Negro shoeshine man, taught him those things. So that by the time Jack reached his middle teens it was said of him that he could whip any man in town. Nor had the years since then improved his disposition.

Having grown up like that, he did not regard himself as coming from Central High School or the University of Virginia. He'd kept himself aloof from those places even while he was attending them. No, he thought of himself as coming from Aycock's and Marguerita's, and believed that his future well-being was more likely to depend on what he'd learned in those places than it would on anything that had been said in a classroom. He wanted to stay in Charlottesville and reestablish the Cabell family. That way he could redeem those of its members who had formed conflicting allegiances during the mysterious absences of his father.

Not that Jack despised the University of Virginia, because he knew that what it had to teach would be of use, too, in a sort of low-level, technical way. He was glad to be going there, and wouldn't have been admitted in the first place if it hadn't been for one of Marguerita's customers, Jefferson Woolworth, the Ford dealer and real estate tycoon. Woolworth, of course, never did something for nothing, and had extracted from Jack a promise that he would stop fooling around with Woolworth's daughter. A promise Jack had made very quickly at the time, because even at eighteen he'd known that fistfighting was the lowest level of conflict and that there were men in town who could whip you much worse in other ways, and that Woolworth, probably, could do almost anything he wanted to him and get away with it.

So Jack's getting into the university had been a fluke, and he'd been almost illiterate when he entered, devoid of any cultural background beyond his urchin's cynical suspicion that the Albemarle County Court House was just a whorehouse with white columns; slightly different tricks, greatly different fees. In short, he was a kind of political scientist.

He'd been obliged to work his way through the University, and had worked very hard. He had an arrangement with his grandfather whereby he would be allowed to live on with the other Cabells so long as he paid for his room, board, tuition, clothes, and books. In addition, he was to contribute a regular amount toward the support of the younger Cabell children; three sisters and one brother. During Christmas week he was allowed to live at the big house free.

Somehow, between his several jobs, he'd found a little time to study, and had gotten through three years of college. Then, to his astonishment, he'd been admitted to the law school, where he was a senior now. During his five years at the university he had never ceased being grateful to Woolworth for teaching him what the limits were, nor

8

breaking his promise about Woolworth's daughter as often as he thought he could get away with it. He was used to living with the furtive knowledge that he might be found out. But there didn't seem to be any other way to live. He wasn't going to give up the girl. She meant a lot to him.

He did not like the bindle stiffs who gathered in front of Aycock's because they tended to remind him of his own situation. It was a long drop from the University of Virginia Law School to the sidewalk out there, but a sudden drop, too. He did not know why they'd circled in on Aycock's. They were like buzzards, to his way of thinking, and he detested them.

Thus when he looked up and saw the big fellow blocking Phoebe's way, it came as a pleasurable opportunity. He didn't even hear what the man was saying, something to the effect that here was a smarter crack than the one they'd been pitching pennies at.

This was how it all began; Jack Cabell, blond, greeneyed, handsome, dressed in a manner well beyond his means, and with the sort of deeply healthy complexion that made you start seeing in colors if you had been seeing only in grays before; Cabell, with the disposition of a cobra, looking up over his poised pool stick and seeing now, as through the sights of a Mauser, the bindle stiff blocking the girl's way, and it was neither business nor chivalry that started him now toward the door with that smooth motion of his, but the other thing, the anger.

Handsomely dressed in a dark-blue suit he was, with his coat off and the rolled-up white sleeves protruding from the vest; moving now past George Gordon, the shoeshine man, and his well-beloved smell of polishes, and out onto the sidewalk's blue twilight, in the shadow of the buildings. As far as Jack was concerned, it could have been any woman, even a grandmother, although there was no question of that, not with the rounded wanton graceful tilt of the hips under the dress. Now as he emerged onto the cool blue sidewalk, they came crowding out behind him, the Negro shoeshine man, his mentor, first, but the rest of them, town boys, mostly, a few town men, too, spilling out onto the sidewalk, forming a circle, knowing as surely as Cabell himself knew what was going to happen next.

He almost killed the fellow who had been blocking her way, cutting his face open in six or seven places, knocking out a tooth, and folding the nose under the left eye as if it had been made of perforated cardboard. Finally he knocked him cold. Cabell wasn't very big, either, maybe one hundred forty-five pounds, five foot nine, barrel-chested and wiry, half a hundred pounds lighter than the man he beat. But there hadn't been any question about the outcome. There had been no more real risk to Cabell than there might have been if he had gone on shooting pool.

Although, of course, Phoebe didn't know that. To her, it was a brave act, and just the sort of thing she had in mind when she thought about honor. It didn't occur to her that her rescuer had come out of the pool hall, let alone that he belonged there.

So she went back to her brother's (or the place that was called her brother's), with her heart beating fast, pleased that the young man had fought for her, and more positive than ever that honor wasn't jailed in old trees and tinted daguerreotypes, but was a living energy of some sort, and attracted to itself. As for the bindle stiff, it was too bad; he had the look of having been a gentleman once. She thought he must have had honor once and lost it.

Phoebe lived out in back of Jefferson Woolworth's mansion in a two-story weathered red brick house called

10

the Slave Quarters, which she shared with her brother Bill and his wife, Colette Woolworth London. Phoebe disliked living at the Slave Quarters and did not feel at home there.

Because life's minimum for her, so far, was to have a place of refuge. She'd always had one when she lived at her father's place at Rappahannock and she'd had one at Barnard, too, until she had moved out of her room into the book-filled apartment of Patrick Henry Roosevelt. Where she had tried to dive down into the books as a sort of refuge, but they weren't the sort of books that could provide that for her and eventually she had run out into the New York traffic, screaming and clawing at her face, and running from Roosevelt, who was trying to teach her things she did not wish to know.

She could stand everything, she believed, if only she could have a small room all her self where she could lock the door and not be bothered. This was doubly important to her now that she believed that Pat Roosevelt might be coming South. She needed a locked room and her brother to protect her.

But Bill wasn't around much. He studied late up at the university, or went to the special parties Colette's friends gave, or else was out playing polo.

Not only was he gone most of the time, but the Slave Quarters seemed entirely penetrable when he was there. It was like living out of doors. Colette's friends came and went as they chose, doors were left open, and people who were strangers to Phoebe would walk in without knocking, fix themselves drinks, and even wander into her room. So, too, could Roosevelt walk in any time he wanted. Anybody could.

Nor was she making any progress in getting out of there. She had been in Charlottesville six weeks now and

11

had not been asked out, certainly not even approached by any of Colette's group, who seemed to have some esoteric interests and spoke an intimate lingo Phoebe did not understand. She could never keep up with them when they were talking about automobiles and polo ponies, and besides, she was ashamed of the secretarial school, and afraid to talk too much. She believed that shorthand and typing were gross pursuits compared to the English literature and music she'd been studying at Barnard.

On the other hand, she had nothing to do with the grease monkeys and house painters the secretarial school girls dated. Thus she felt herself caught in an uninhabited middle land, working hard for no lovely purpose and not even safe; her sanity not even safe; for if Roosevelt had done it to her before, presumably he could do it again; and if being without privacy could do it, she was once more on the edge. Although, thank God, it was Charlottesville, Virginia, not New York City, and there was some mint smell to mingle with the train smoke. She loved those smells commingled. In Charlottesville one could have just enough of the city mixed with just enough of the country, and if the other thing, meeting the young man, could only begin to work, everything would be okay, or so she believed.

Now, as she came up the flagstone walkway by Woolworth's place, she saw that another party was in progress. Out in the bricked courtyard young couples were dancing to radio music. There were rose-colored paper lanterns and they threw their light on the underside of what fall leaves remained. A white-jacketed Negro was serving drinks on a silver tray. The doors to the Slave Quarters stood open. A couple was standing in the doorway, kissing, and it wasn't until Phoebe had passed them and gone into the house that she realized the girl was Colette. Her

12

mouth had been open and Phoebe had seen the young man's tongue going in. There were very many people inside the Slave Quarters. It was dark in there and thick with cigarette smoke and the smell of alcohol. Everyone seemed to be drinking.

She opened the door to her room and saw a couple on the bed. The girl's dress was up around her waist and the young man had his hand between her legs. She closed the door and went to stand alone in the dark part of the hallway. When the couple emerged she saw that the young man was her brother. She went in her room, closed the door, and began to straighten out the bed. Then the smell came over her and she began to gag. She went to the window, opened it, and stood there gulping air. Across the alley the big Cabell house was beginning to be lit up now that dusk was coming on.

Phoebe had met one of the Cabell girls, although she had not been over to the house. It was a big, rambling white clapboard place with dark-green shutters and trim; it looked more like a boardinghouse than a mansion. She wished it were a boardinghouse. She wished she could live there. Sometimes she'd thought she would sell some of the evening dresses Colette had given her and use the money to get a room somewhere else. But there was something wrong with that, too. She stood there at the open window, looking out across the cobblestoned alley to the Cabell house, whose many windows shone now with golden light.

One of the doors to her room, the one that was kept locked, led to the kitchen, and through it she heard two young men talking.

"We are every one of us going to be killed in the war," one of them said.

"What war?" the other one said.

"You just wait and see."

She stretched out on top of her bed and fell asleep. When she woke up it was fully night. Someone was crawling in the darkness across the floor.

"What is it?" she said.

"It's I," her brother said. Before marrying Colette Woolworth, he'd have said, "It's me."

She sat up in bed and saw him crawling there and smelled the aroma of whiskey.

"Lost my wrist watch. Here it is." He stood up and strapped on the watch. He walked over to the door, opened it a crack, and light speared in, blinding her.

"Pat Roosevelt called," he said.

"I don't want to talk to him."

"He's over at the Monticello Hotel."

"Stay here, then," she said.

"I can't. There's an Honor Council meeting tonight. I'm a member now, you know."

"Then let me come with you."

"I can't," her brother said. "It's secret. We are going to discuss some pretty serious things."

She didn't say anything.

"He's not going to bother you," her brother said. "He's a gentleman."

Patrick Henry Roosevelt had been in Charlottesville for three days. He had come down to persuade Phoebe to marry him, although he was here for other things as well. He was an orderly young man and took one thing at a time. He was attending a conference of Southern writers at the University of Virginia. He himself planned to be a Southern writer one day. He'd interviewed Mrs. Glasgow and a little fellow from Mississippi whose name he hadn't gotten and had spent a lot of time exploring the grounds. He felt he knew a lot about Mr. Jefferson's university. He was working on his doctorate in Southern history, just finishing up. He wasn't from the South.

He'd wandered around the Lawn, poked through the Ranges, gazed at the Rotunda, and spent an hour in Edgar Allan Poe's old room, meditating. He had gone through the rare-book room of the Alderman Library and sipped mint juleps at a garden party given for visiting scholars on a patio inside the serpentine walls. He knew a great deal about the South, he thought.

That had taken him through yesterday. He'd spent today up at Monticello, Mr. Jefferson's residence, in the company of an old old darky named Doc, a former slave who was a bellhop at the Monticello Hotel (which was back in Charlottesville itself, not up here on Jefferson's little mountain).

Pat had rented the old Negro from the hotel to carry his picnic hamper and to talk to. And he was having a good time with Doc, whose tales of nineteenth-century life in Virginia made him worth having, whatever the hotel was charging for him; although as for that, Pat had not asked how much it would be. It was bad form, he believed, to talk about money or even think about it. It distracted one's mind from the important things. He was fond of the old darky.

He'd spent the day going methodically through Jefferson's mansion, and now it was late afternoon, dusk, and he was down by the Jefferson graveyard, having finally remembered to eat. He had the Negro break out a repast of cold fried chicken and dry white wine. Then, inviting the old man to join him, he listened to some more of Doc's stories. He recorded them in his pocket notebook, using one of the Randolph tombstones for a writing table. The notebook had been given him by his father, and

15

stamped in gold on the cover were the initials PR.

This notebook had been given to his father by a South Carolina neighbor. So the PR stood for Piotr Rosenfeld, his father. Although his own name was Patrick Henry Roosevelt. He'd had the Patrick from the beginning— that was after his Irish grandfather. His father, who was very patriotic, had added the Henry from a name he'd learned in the Americanization school. And Pat himself had changed the last name to Roosevelt, the year he turned twenty-one, after Teddy Roosevelt, who'd been a friend of his father's.

He had two older brothers. The eldest was going to run the asbestos plant and the next one had been launched by the father into New York City politics. But it seemed that the parents hadn't any special expectations for Pat. So he was able to follow his natural bent. He was a scholarly fellow, and tended quite naturally toward academe. By now, at twenty-four, he had succeeded in almost everything he'd tried to do, and if he could be said to have a general want, it was to be considered a plain, ordinary American, on an equal footing with everybody else. Indeed, one of the few things in life that moved him to anger—for he was gentle-natured and dreamy—was having his denials of Jewishness rejected. It was unfair, he thought. He was an American agnostic, period.

His father, whom he respected, still maintained a love for the old country and a strict adherence to the rituals and dietary practices of Orthodox Judaism. And Pat, not wishing to upset him, had kept the agnosticism private, participating in festivals whenever asked and eating what was put in front of him. He did not wish to hurt anybody's feelings, if he could help it, and was known among his friends as a tactful young man. Thus he'd aroused no parental resentment when he changed his name. His father had even held a party in honor of the occasion.

Pat was a handsome fellow, six feet tall, with the curly black hair of his Irish ancestors. He was squarejawed and athletic, and there was a healthy, ruddy look about him. He had a firm, wide mouth, alert blue eyes, and moved with muscular grace. Three years previously, he'd wrestled for the United States in the 178-pound class in the Olympic Games, and had brought home the bronze medal from Amsterdam.

Now, his day at Monticello ended, he dropped a ten-dollar gold piece into the darky's pink palm and walked slowly up the hill from the cemetery, taking his time so that the wheezing old fellow could keep up.

It made him feel good to have someone around who was faithful to him. Indeed, that was the prime quality he was looking for in a wife (that and good looks). Not that she'd be obliged to be his slave. But Pat prized faithfulness, so it was going to be a Southern girl or nothing—this Southern girl. He had accepted the likelihood that there would be a rival by now—she was far too beautiful, he thought, for there not to be one—and he would do whatever was necessary to win her back. He would even fight for her, if he had to, and he would do it like the Southerners did. Thus Patrick Henry Roosevelt, a rather lonely young man, in love with the South and ready to take a wife.

He knew, of course, that Phoebe feared the North, was devastated by it. But he no longer wished to take her there. He had better plans now, and on the basis of them, and on the strength of having been her first lover, he nourished a reasonable certainty of success. He was convinced he knew her better than she knew herself.

Coming up the hill from the graveyard, with the basket-toting old darky toiling along behind him now, Pat looked down the mountain and saw that some of the electric lights of Charlottesville had already come on. It was only twilight down there, however; whereas in the graveyard hollow from which the old Negro was emerging it was already night. The old man moved very slowly and was the same color as that night, almost as if he'd come from one of the graves. And Pat stood there waiting for him and snapping his fingers; quietly, so as not to seem to be summoning up the old man. Snap, snap, snap; the pace, the pace, the pace. Sometimes it was so slow that it made you want to slit your throat. Well, that was one thing you would have to do for yourself, down here as elsewhere. Anything else they would do for you. He was impatient to see Phoebe, to do whatever had to be done.

When Jack Cabell got home the big house was quiet. There was only the sound of the mantel clock in the parlor, ticking. His grandmother was in there reading.

The old lady saw him and closed the book. It was a worn black-leather Bible that had been given her on her tenth birthday by General Stonewall Jackson, a cousin of hers. She cherished this Bible and liked to read it in the quietude of the parlor.

"Have you seen my father?" Jack asked. He always said it that way. Everybody else in this house called his mother's father by that name. Jack's father came home only on rare weekends. He worked down in Louisa, Virginia.

"He will be along soon, I expect," his grandmother said.

"Didn't he come in on the bus?"

"Is it that late?" she asked.

"Yes, ma'm."

"I lose track of time. Come here and give me a kiss."

He walked over now and kissed her. She smelled faintly of a perfume he remembered from earliest boyhood. On the table by her chair was a copy of *Presbyterian Life.* It had an article on "The Sin of the Jews."

She patted the arm of her chair and he sat down there beside her.

"You are too big to sit on my lap any more," the old lady said.

"Yes, ma'm."

"I will bet you have been up to something. I can always tell when you have been up to something."

"No."

"You look poorly," his grandmother said.

"No," Jack said. "I am all right."

She patted him on the knee. "Are you still my boy?"

"Yes, ma'm."

Her hand emerged from under the shawl now, holding a fifty-cent piece, and she took hold of his hand and pressed the money into his palm. "This is for something special," she said.

"I can't take this."

"You hush up. Your grandmother knows what a hard time you've had."

He went upstairs. The doors to his sisters' rooms stood open and he saw the usual pink garments, jars of cosmetics on tables, photographs of young men, powder puffs. It was strange that the rooms were empty because it was dusk now and their dates would be calling for them. The two oldest ones went out with university boys and their mother was proud of them for that.

Jack went into the bathroom, closed the door and locked it, and stood in front of the mirror in the near-darkness. I cannot recognize myself, he thought.

Now he switched on the electric light bulb and inspected his hand, his left hand at the third knuckle, where a tooth-shaped flap of skin had been torn back like a tab.

It was still bleeding and the blood had flowed down over the shield of his Cabell coat-of-arms ring and caked there. He removed the ring and washed it very carefully. Then he took down his father's styptic pencil and applied it to the cut and stopped the bleeding and put the ring back on.

His hands were getting soft, and this annoyed him. For years he had soaked his hands in brine several hours a week, and thought now that if he had kept on doing that, the tooth would have snapped off instead of cutting the skin. He had begun the business with the brine because the heavyweight champion of the world, Jack Dempsey, did that. Now Dempsey had not been champion for five years, and Jack was disquieted by this. He had grown up accustomed to genuine champions.

It was quiet when he emerged into the second-floor hallway. He went to his father's room and knocked on the door. There was no answer. All that could be heard was the soft ticking of the clock in the parlor below. He had almost reached the stairs when they pounced on him out of he knew not where, possibly the broom closet, or the linen closet, or both, but he was flat on his face being pummeled and tickled before he had a chance to think about where they came from and he fought back now with his usual desperate, silent determination as they had his arms pinned to the floor and his face smudged down into the carpet, as they tickled him and squealed and giggled and mussed his hair and rumpled his suit and goosed him and pinched him, and as one of them was pummeling him in the head with a pillow. And now, freeing one hand, he began to pinch out blackly, despairingly, at the womanflesh which was his own flesh and which had tormented him and driven him to the attic in the first place, not for lack of space but for lack of patience and out of the fear that one day by God they would go too far and he would kill every damn one of them. Now, freeing the other arm, he caught one of them by the waist and turning brought her down with him. He was being pummeled in the face with the pillow and the tickling was getting very bad indeed and they were rubbing something on his ears, that was it, they were coloring his ears red with the lipstick again as now he reached out and grabbed the offending tube and flung it down the stairwell muttering God damn you between his teeth too silent to be heard and fighting with all his might and bitterly. Then he was released. Alone, struggling to get up, as the three sisters' three doors slammed in unison, and lock! lock! lock! as he leaped to his feet and rushed red-eared and disheveled toward the nearest door, which was, locked!

Bitterly, silently, he went into the bathroom and washed his ears, saying nothing, listening not at all to the cooings now coming from behind the thick oak doors. "Jack!? Has oo got a date tonight, Jaaack?" "Did oo mess oo hair up? Poooor Jaaaack." Scrubbing very hard so that when the ears were clean they were almost as red from the blood rushing there as they had been from the lipstick in the first place, and recovering his dignity and the integrity of his wardrobe, and the part in the middle of his hair, he went downstairs with the dignity of a cat and with no other sign of what had happened than the red and glowing ears.

In the kitchen, his mother was standing plumply in front of the stove, a greasy spatula in her hand. She turned and grabbed him to herself with the spatula upraised and dripping.

"Where is my father?" he asked.

"I expect he will be along next week," she said. She was a cheerful, plump woman with long auburn hair.

"Maybe he missed the bus," Jack said.

She was looking him up and down.

"Where are you going, you young scalawag?" she asked.

"I've got a date," he said.

"That's good," his mother said. "You work too hard. You ought to have a good time."

"I'm going to have a good time," he said.

"You had better let me give you something to eat."

"No, thanks," he said. He had been upset lately. He did not feel like eating.

"Dot and Jinna are going up to the university tonight," she said.

"Where?"

"The AEP."

"That's what I thought."

Now Jack's oldest sister, Dot, came into the kitchen. She turned her back to him and leaned back to have her dress's nape snapped. He did what she wanted.

"Did you get a postcard from Dad?" he asked.

"Yes, silly." She turned around to him. She was a pretty girl and looked like her mother.

"How do you like my new dress?" she asked. It was a translucent powder-blue dress with rhinestones sewn in front. The kitchen was thick with the smell of cooking meat.

"Is he coming?"

"No." She was posing for him. "You still haven't said what you think of the dress."

"It's all right," he said.

"Colette Woolworth brought it over," Jack's mother said.

"Honestly," Dot said, "when are you and Jack going to learn it isn't Woolworth any more?"

Jack opened the porch door and beckoned to his sister. "I want to talk to you," he said.

"No. I'm not going out there with you again."

"This will just take a second," he said.

"No. If you have anything to tell me you can say it in front of Mother."

He grabbed her arm and pushed her out on the porch and closed the door. It was dark out here. There was music coming from across the alley.

"I thought I told you not to do that," he said.

She opened her mouth to scream and he grabbed her and bent her back, holding his hand over her mouth.

"Listen," he said. "I will be goddamned if I will have you taking charity from that slut."

Dot was glaring at him with wide eyes. Then she went limp and he let go of her.

"You are a Cabell of Virginia," he said. He stood there looking at her in the glow of the alley light. She was half turned away, her face hidden by shadow.

"I don't know why you treat me like this," she said. "You know we can't afford things."

"Yes, we can."

"You're not being practical," she said.

"Practical be damned."

She shook her head. "No."

"Listen," Jack said. "You are about the prettiest girl in town. You don't have to go out with fellows like that."

Her face was in the light again and she was looking at him calmly.

"I don't know, Jack," she said. "When we were young we used to get along, but I expect we'll spend the rest of our lives not knowing each other very well."

"Don't talk like that," he said.

"It's true. We just don't understand each other."

"We have got to understand each other," he said. "I will be head of the family some day."

She reached up, straightened out his coat lapel. "Listen, Jack," she said. "I am sorry about Colette."

"There is nothing to be sorry about."

"I truly am."

"I didn't bring you out here to talk about that. I brought . . ."

"Why?"

"I forget," he said. He had been having trouble concentrating. "I don't want you to go out with fellows like that."

"I have to be practical, Jack. You can be a Cabell of Virginia for as long as you like. But I am going to be a Cohen of New Jersey."

His mother came out on the porch.

"Sid is here," she said.

Jack went past her and into the house, toward the very back, where the smoking room was, where the women never came. His mother's father was sitting in the red leather armchair, smoking a cigar. A drink of golden whiskey, with a little red cherry in it, stood by his elbow. He was reading the *Daily Progress*. He always kept up with current events. He was a stocky, vigorous, redfaced old man.

"May I use the car?" Jack asked.

"No."

"I want to go and get my father. He missed the bus, I think."

"No, he didn't," the old man said.

"I want to go and get him all the same."

"What if he doesn't want you to get him?"

Jack didn't say anything.

The old man was looking up over the top of the newspaper, blue eyes above black bombers. The eyes looked younger than the rest of him, Jack thought.

The old man winked.

"I don't believe any of that stuff," Jack said.

"Well, you can't use the car. And you owe for the room and board."

"That isn't due until tomorrow."

"Just make sure you pay on time," his grandfather said. "I want you to learn how to live up to your responsibilities before you go out in the world."

"I am already out in the world," Jack said.

"No you aren't," the old man said. "And somebody has got to teach you." He returned to the newspaper.

Jack went out in the back yard. It was dark there except for the leafshrouded alley light and the pink glow coming from Woolworth's garden. The garage stood mute, with moonlight shining bluely on its roof. A man in a white shirt was leaning up against the garage. The man's cigarette glowed bright orange, dulled. Now it flipped out, arching into the alleyway. It was the Negro George Gordon, who always wore a starched fresh white shirt, and this one shone now in the moonlight and Jack's nostrils caught the acrid smell of the French cigarette the man smoked. Gauloises. Jack smoked them too, copying Gordon.

"I got the papers," the Negro said.

"Why bring them here?" Jack said.

"Got to," the Negro said. "Police been asking questions." He thrust the papers into Jack's hand.

"What questions?"

"About those."

"That's none of their business," Jack said. "That's university business."

"I don't know nothing about that," Gordon said. "I got to go." He walked off abruptly down the alley with the moonglow on his starched shirt growing dimmer and smaller, and disappeared at last down the hill, where curved car fenders gleamed in the streetlight.

Jack admired Gordon and could not imagine what his life would be like if the Negro hadn't taught him how to fight and how to handle himself in other ways that had nothing to do with overt fighting. He owed it to Gordon that he'd been able to stay in Charlottesville as long as he had, and was proud of being on intimate terms with a criminal. Although he was enough of a criminal himself by now not to boast of it to anyone. Gordon, in turn, had learned from the older, darker Negro who performed abortions and who owned part of Marguerita's and several other business establishments on Vinegar Hill as well. It was what one of the professors at the university might have called an oral tradition, Jack supposed, and he liked to imagine that when he got older he would pass on what he had learned to his son. That was how the professors had said the oral tradition worked. There was another kind of oral tradition the whores had, but Jack supposed the professors weren't referring to that.

An owl hooted. There was a family of them in the hemlock tree by the garage and sometimes Jack would see one of them perched on the electricity wire under the alley light.

He was alone in the back yard, in the deep shadows. He sat down on the bench by the goldfish pond and lit a Gauloise. He lit the cigarette the way Gordon did, cupping his hand even when the wind wasn't blowing.

His knees were still trembling from the fight with the bindle stiff. He found he trembled more after fights now.

27

He had this desire to keep hitting his man after he'd won, and this frightened him. Sometimes he even thought he would like to kill somebody.

Sometimes he would put himself to sleep by daydreaming about killing. The victim was always somebody who had gotten in his way. He tried to be scrupulous about choosing the victims, and picked only those who had thwarted what he believed to be legitimate desires. Because he did not want so much out of life anyway, he believed. Only very simple things: to live in Virginia as eight generations of his fathers had, to do honest work, and not be violated. But he had found that it took extraordinary efforts to achieve these simple things, and often he failed.

At the University of Virginia, where money ruled, he'd found that the only way to avoid being snubbed was to stay aloof and keep his mouth shut. This had gone against his nature at first, because he'd been outgoing and gregarious to begin with, like his father. But most people who knew him now regarded him as a profoundly cold young man.

And the honesty had had to be abandoned. At least it had seemed necessary to Jack to abandon some of it, because he had to work five days a week, ten hours a day of manual labor at the laundry plant, plus two nights a week at the other place, and could not keep up with the law school studies. Thus he had managed to stay in school only by purchasing advance copies of the examinations. The necessity of doing that had lacerated his conscience, and to make up for it he used his summers and holidays to study up in his attic room. He loved the study of law and wished he had more time.

As for not being violated, there didn't seem to be any way out of that, either, because he was patronized by the

law school professors and harassed by the laundry fore-
man, who disliked him because he was a "college boy."

What had made these things tolerable to Jack was his
conviction that there was no way out of them. If he could
put up with all that until he graduated from law school,
things might be different, although, even then, there was
a great uncertainty because of the Depression and because having clients in Charlottesville meant having contacts with moneyed people. But he was looking forward
to being a lawyer because it would be a new kind of fight.
He was tired of this old fight. It had been going on for
many years now and he was desperate to regain control
of the Cabell family before it was too late.

There was a pink glow on the underside of the leaves
overhanging Woolworth's garden and radio music float-
ing over the brick wall. He was used to music and laughter
coming from over there.

He sat there on the bench, running his fingertips along
the cool marble inscription carved in the back, the family
motto: "Faithful and Grateful." He had bought the
bench when they'd auctioned off the old Cabell plantation. It had belonged to his great-great-great-grandfather,
and was the only thing he had from the old family. The
signet ring was new, having been made to order at a
genealogical jewelry house in Baltimore. Jack was fond of
his ring, but he liked the bench even better and wished
he had a place to put it.

The radio music and laughter got momentarily louder
as, across the alley, the garden door opened and closed.
There was a glow of pink light and then darkness again
and a girl was standing there in the alley under the hemlock tree. A low whistle came.

He didn't answer. Lately he had found that the whistle
made him nervous, although he could not tell why. Pres-

ently the girl came around the bushes and went to stand under his attic window. Jack was hidden by the bushes. The low whistle came again.

"Colette."

"I knew I saw you," she said.

"I am here, all right."

"Who were you talking to?"

"It was nobody," he said. "Just a nigger."

"You aren't hiding from me, are you?" Her hand clutched at his sleeve.

"No."

"Isn't it strange," she said. "When it's nighttime I can see you, but you can't see me. In the daytime it's the other way around."

She had passed him as she went into a jewelry store earlier that day and had not spoken. Which had something to do with why he had been so angry at the pool hall.

"Remember when I used to bring you favors?" she said.

"Yes," he said. That had been during his freshman year, before he'd gotten a job to pay for the board. Then he had begun making some money and bought a jar of peanut butter and a loaf of bread and quit eating the party favors. He had never liked them anyway, even when he was very hungry. That was the year Colette came out. She had come out in that garden over there and Jack had sat at his attic window eating a peanut butter sandwich, watching.

"Let's go upstairs," he said.

"No," she murmured.

"We can go up the back way."

She shook her head. She was a good-looking girl and tended slightly toward plumpness. She had sweet-smelling hair, usually, and he tried now to smell it but there was a perfume he did not like. He had liked the way it smelled when she was thirteen and had used nothing but soap. She was standing very close to him now, pushed up softly against his arm.

"Did you let him have you again?" Jack asked.

"Please," she said.

"God damn it, I asked you a question."

"Please, Jack. If I am going to be honest with you, you'll have to stop cross-examining me."

"You shouldn't let him trap you," Jack said.

"You are acting like a prosecuting attorney," she said.

He was very angry.

"You should leave the door open or something," he said. "You shouldn't let him trap you."

She put her arms around him. "If we're going to be honest with one another," she said, "you're going to have to stop being so rough on me."

"I am not the one who is rough on you," he said.

"Some night I'll come out and you won't be here," she said.

"No," Jack said. "We will both be here. Even after we're dead."

"You'll grow old in Cincinnati or Denver or someplace like that," she said. "You won't like me any more."

Jack didn't say anything. Thinking, You may be right about the not liking you any more, because when it comes to that, maybe I didn't like you as much as I thought to begin with. But you are not going to Cincinnati or Denver me, because I am a Cabell of Virginia or I am nothing.

"We've got to stop," Colette said. She was hugging him as she said this. She had been doing this for ten years now and at first Jack had enjoyed it in an uncomplicated way. Even now when she hugged him he could remember when it had been like that.

31

The best thing would be to kill you, he thought. Then you wouldn't remember any more what he did to you. But London would remember and I would have to kill him, too. Then I would remember. But I am not going to kill myself because it would mean he killed me with that thing between his legs, whereas now it is only violation. I would like to kill somebody, though.

3

The mantel clock was striking nine when Jack walked into Marguerita's to begin his night's work. Half a dozen of the university boys were already in the front parlor, passing a flask around. They nodded to him and proffered the flask, but Jack shook his head. It was dangerous to drink and work. None of the girls was there. Jack heard their squeals coming from the back parlor, where the businessmen sported.

"Have you all paid?" he asked.

"Hell, Jack, it looks like there isn't going to be anything to pay for," a tall blond fellow said. This was a young man whose father owned coal mines in Pennsylvania. He was reaching for his wallet as he said it.

"They'll be along in a little while," Jack said. It was going to be a busy night. It was a football weekend. Virginia was playing Sewanee.

"Are you ready for the exam?" the blond fellow asked. There were a lot of bills in his wallet, twenties and fifties, and he was having trouble finding smaller denominations. He was in Jack's legal ethics class.

"As ready as I'm going to be," Jack said.

"I can't figure it out," the blond fellow said. "It's too damned subjective, if you ask me. I'd rather be back in contracts, something I can get my teeth into."

"They will be along in a little while," Jack said. He collected the money from the students and took it down the hall to Marguerita's office. A dozen years ago, when Jack had begun coming here, this had been her working room, and she'd handled the cash on top of the dresser between her own appointments. Since then she'd gotten in more girls and had even been obliged to open up a sort of shed out back—which had once been a horse stable, then a garage, and now was a whorehouse annex upstairs, and downstairs something else. Her personal customers had been cut back to one man, Jefferson Woolworth. She was making a lot of money, and no one knew what she did with it. There were even rumors that she buried it someplace.

Jack stood there while she counted the money. There were pulp magazines spread out all over the room, which George Gordon, her husband, fetched up from Main Street, where he bought the out-of-date ones from Old Man Gathright, Jack's grandfather, who ran the News Store. The room gave off an overpowering sensation of pinkness: the walls, the bedcovers, the chairs, the lampshade, all were pink; and there was a paper lantern of that color encircling the naked electric light bulb in the ceiling. Which formerly had dominated the room. So Marguerita was picking up culture from somewhere, although whether from the romance magazines, or Woolworth, or whatever, no one knew. She was pretty close-mouthed.

She was sitting now at the ancient roll-top desk she'd bought from the estate of old Judge Dabney when he died. She was wearing her translucent green eyeshade and counting the money. A mulatto woman of fifty or fifty-five who had been beautiful once, she still carried with her the poise of that beauty. She was plump, with black, slick, artificially straightened hair and eyebrows almost bald and filled in with some kind of pencil that was also purchased from the news store. Her eyes as she looked up at him now were a startling light blue, set in a face turned green by the eyeshade.

"Listen here," she said. "You in trouble?"

"No."

There was a knock at the door and George Gordon came in, accompanied by the Doctor, an old, very black, hunchbacked Negro in the blue and gold bellhop uniform of the Monticello Hotel.

"Key to the manger," Gordon said. That was what the whores called the big downstairs room at the shed. Gordon had one of the French cigarettes dangling from the corner of his mouth. His eyes were squinted up against the smoke and he stood there peering at the soft stacks of lime-colored money as Marguerita fished in a cubbyhole for the key.

"Clean off the bed while you're waiting," she said.

Gordon, without removing the cigarette from the corner of his mouth, began to do as he was told. Then Jack knew Woolworth was there. Meanwhile the Doctor, who was so black he shone blue, stood there walleyed and wheezing and staring at the floor and the baseboard all at the same time. He made a little soughing noise when he breathed. He was carrying some straightened-out wire coat hangers in his fat jeweled hand.

Gordon made neat stacks of the romance magazines, put them on the dresser, and turned back the covers of the bed. Finally Marguerita found the key and tossed it to him and the two Negroes left.

"What is it?" Jack asked.

"I don't want no part of it," Marguerita said.

There was a knock at the hall door. One of the girls, the young, pretty one, came in. She had her hand clasped to her forehead and blood was oozing out between her fingers and running down the back of her hand. Jack had known her all his life. He had never spoken to her but he had watched her growing up. She had been a pretty child and was always neat and wore clean dresses. Her mother worked down at the laundry. Jack had seen her running down Vinegar Hill's steep streets, or skipping rope, or carrying her book satchel home from the nigger school. She was a beautiful young woman and could almost pass for white. He would murmur hello to her in the halls.

Out front more university students were arriving and Jack went among them collecting their money and stuffing it in the side pocket of his jacket.

Suddenly there was a commotion on the porch and Jack went out there. A student was vomiting over the rail into the shrubbery. Two more students stood behind him, watching.

"It's his first time," one of them said.

"Get him out of here," Jack said.

"He'll be all right. He just took too much to drink."

"Get him out of here," Jack said. He did not mind the vomiting because a lot of vomiting went on here and he was used to it. But the boy looked about sixteen and Marguerita liked them to be a couple of years older than that. It was some sort of arrangement she'd worked out with the police and the university. Of course, the girls could come here at any age they wanted, and there was even a twelve-year-old who was the favorite of a hardware dealer. But the girls were another matter.

Down the alley Jack saw a clot of businessmen leaving

by the side door. They always came on weekends. The professors came during the week. These businessmen were laughing and talking, limned against the yellow light that shone out of the manger and threw their shadows across the alley's ancient cobblestones.

Two more students, wearing white coats with stethoscopes stuck down in the pockets, walked up on the porch, paid him, and went in. Jack heard the laughter of the girls coming into the front parlor now, and the squeak of stairs as couples went up to the second floor. He lit a cigarette and looked down the hill toward Main Street. He was just twelve streetlights away from the one in front of his grandfather's store.

Coming through the house again, he saw Jefferson Woolworth sitting on the sofa in the back parlor. He was alone, and wearing a little pink, pointed party hat. Woolworth was a tall, heavy man with a long, flat face, bushy black eyebrows, rimless spectacles. He held up a half-full bottle of whiskey and shook it.

"I have got to work," Jack said.

Woolworth didn't say anything, just went on shaking the bottle and looking at him gimlet-eyed from under bushy brows.

"Do you want something?" Jack asked. But Woolworth didn't reply.

Jack closed the door and returned to the front parlor. Already some students were beginning to come down, tucking in shirttails. Others were going up and passed those on the steps. After the first shift the girls stayed upstairs. There were more students crowding in the front door and Jack stood to the side of it, taking the money.

"She wants to see you," one of the girls said. She pinched him in passing.

Jack went back to the office. The two women were

37

there. The young mulatto was sitting on the bed. She had a fresh white bandage over her eye. Marguerita was seated at the desk, holding a piece of ice up to the side of her head, at the temple. Her face was swollen there and a rivulet of water ran glistening down her tan cheek and dripped off her chin onto a stack of one-dollar bills.

"Mr. Woolworth didn't mean to do nothing," the girl said. "It was just his ring done caught me." She was trying to take Woolworth away from Marguerita. She wanted to open up her own place.

"Listen, honey," Marguerita said. "He is always going to tell you stuff like that. Don't mind about what he tells you, mind what he does." The side of her face was badly swollen.

"I'd leave town," Marguerita told Jack.

"The hell with him," Jack said.

He stepped out in the back alley and stood there listening to the night sounds, crickets and the low hum of rubber tires. When he'd been a baby in his crib it had been the rattle of wagon wheels, clop of hooves. But he seldom heard those sounds any more. A low train whistle came now from down at the yards. Yellow light shone from the manger door. Someone was moaning in there. Jack could see the Doctor's shadow moving like the last fumbling fingers of the tide across the amber cobblestones. In the black strip between buildings, the stars shone dully. They are shining brighter than this where my father is, Jack thought. He missed his father. When he came back in, Marguerita was sitting on the sofa next to Woolworth, who had taken off his glasses. He was kissing the raised place by her eye.

"That will make it well," he said.

She stood up and he slapped her on the fanny. He still had the party hat on. It was tilted back on his head and

38

the little elastic band made an indentation in the flesh under his chin. Now he fished in his pocket and extracted a dollar bill.

"Give that to the girl," he said to Marguerita. "And send me a radio in here. I want to listen to some music. Don't you want to listen to some music, boy?"

"I've got to work."

"Naw you don't," Woolworth said. "You have been too busy, I think." He grabbed Marguerita, dragged her down on his lap, and kissed the side of her head where it was swollen. Jack stood there looking at them. Woolworth's eyes watched him over the top of her slick black hair.

"You like music, don't you, boy?" Woolworth said.

Marguerita floundered to her feet and made for the door.

"Sit down," Woolworth said.

Jack sat in the chair opposite him. He was frightened. Marguerita closed the door, muffling the sound of young laughter. Jack and Woolworth were alone now. Up above them springs squeaked and went on squeaking.

Woolworth poured out a tumblerful of whiskey and handed it to him.

"Listen, boy," he said. "Did you ever feel pain?"

"Sure," Jack said.

The older man took off the party hat, put it on the table beside him, and smoothed out his hair with his hand. He had slick brown hair, parted in the middle. "How would you like to spend your fifty-third birthday in a nigger whorehouse?" he said.

"I wouldn't mind," Jack said. "I have spent the last twelve of them here, more or less."

"What about when you are fifty-three?" Woolworth asked. His wife had gone back to her family in France.

"I never get a chance to think that far ahead." Jack took a swallow of whiskey. It was good whiskey.

"Never get a chance, huh?" Woolworth asked. "That sounds like some kind of whining to me."

Jack hadn't meant it that way. What he had meant was, simply, that he lived from day to day. He did not mind that kind of living, actually, and supposed he would always do it. They had discussed this point once in a philosophy class at the university.

He was listening to the rapid squeaking of the springs and thinking to himself how good they must sound to Marguerita, since every squeak meant money. These were coming from the young girl's room. Five cents a squeak, something like that. Well, that young one would be worth it. Jack had wanted her for a long time. Just once so that he would have something good to remember.

"I gave you a lot of chances," Woolworth said.

Presently Marguerita brought the radio and plugged it in by the old gas fixture. It was a wooden radio with a pointed arch.

"You want to listen to some music?" Woolworth asked.

"No," Jack said. He sipped at the whiskey.

"You listen to it with niggers all the time," Woolworth said. "You might as well listen to it with a white man."

Jack's heart was beating fast.

"You don't mind associating with a white man every now and then, I suppose," Woolworth said. He switched on the radio and sat there peering into it.

"It is either the niggers or it is some white woman you have got no business with," Woolworth said. "You haven't had to deal with a white man. That is one of the reasons you don't know anything about pain."

The radio was shaped like a witch's cottage. The dial was the door. At last the golden light began to glow. It was the same color of light that came out of the manger. Piano music emerged. "All Alone."

"I can find you some of your nigger music if you want," Woolworth said.

"No, thanks."

"Maybe you broke your arm or had a toothache once," Woolworth said. "But you don't know what pain is." He was a big, tall man who played a lot of golf out at the Farmington Country Club and his body wasn't as fat as his face said it was going to be.

"I know you been buying your examination questions from one of them nighttime niggers at the law school," Woolworth said.

Jack felt his face getting red and he made himself concentrate on saying nothing; having learned ten years ago at Aycock's that the most important time not to talk was when your mouth wanted to.

"Sort of makes you scared, doesn't it?" Woolworth said. He turned up the radio. "How do you like the music now?" he asked.

"It's all right," Jack said.

"I notice there is always music coming from over at that place of yours."

"Well," Jack said, "there is music coming from both of our places."

"There must be some special times when you play the music," Woolworth said. "Like when you have a guest over."

"I have kept my bargain," Jack said.

"Like you did on the examinations."

"I will give you my word of honor."

Woolworth shook his head, slowly. "No," he said. "A man without money has not got a word. He will lie, and sneak, and cheat, and break his promises, and do anything

41

he thinks he can get by with to get his money. Then, after he has got enough, he can have a word if he wants to. Listen, son. You are going to school with rich boys. What do they call it, the honor system?"

"Yes."

"That is a rich-boy system, son. Listen, a man will kill for his daughter." And he slouched there longleggedly on his spine, staring across at Jack.

"You are doing it to *me,*" Woolworth said.

The door swung open and there against the chiaroscuro of the hallway shining pinkly in cake-candle glow was Marguerita in her silken dress.

"Get that thing out of here," Woolworth said. Marguerita backed out of sight and the hand that came forward to close the door was a police officer's with gold trimming on the cuff.

"I am going to do it to you," Woolworth said. "How do you like that music?"

"What do you want?" Jack asked. His voice was tight in his throat, high-pitched.

"It isn't a question of what I want," Woolworth said. "It's a question of what I'm going to do. I am going to ruin you."

"You just tell me what I can do," Jack said.

"What if I pull down my trousers and tell you to kiss my ass?" Woolworth said.

"I would do it."

"Spotswood!" Woolworth yelled out. The door opened and the police chief came in. Back of him, leaning up against the wall, Marguerita stood there holding the cake with the candles half burned down. There were a lot of candles. The police chief was a muscular, blackhaired fellow, six foot four. He came and stood in front of the radio, looking down at Jack.

"I got a young fellow here says he wants to kiss my ass."

The chief grinned, looking down at Jack, and his eyes didn't grin.

"Just joking," Jack said.

"Yeah, I bet you were," the chief said.

The door opened and the young girl, the one with the bandage, stood there with her hip wantonly tilted, tying the sash about her waist.

"You want that?" Woolworth asked. The police chief shook his head. "Later."

"I been telling Jack here you got to be fifty-three years old to feel pain," Woolworth said. "Ain't that right?"

The police chief nodded. He was standing in front of the radio and the music came out from around him.

The girl stood in the doorway looking at them and in the dimness of the hall might almost have been white. The golden light like a nimbus came up behind her and it was Marguerita, with new candles on the cake now, pushing past.

"Get on out of here, boy," the police chief said.

As Jack was leaving he saw Woolworth pulling Marguerita down to kiss the swollen eye and she was trying to balance herself so as not to spill the cake.

All that night, as he went about his job, Jack kept thinking that he might be called to the back parlor and told what to do. But nobody called him and the customers kept coming and in the middle of it Jack saw Woolworth and Marguerita, leaning together and stumbling down the hall to the office that was about to become her bedroom, hitting up against first one wall then the other, and George Gordon standing there with the cigarette dangling out of his mouth and his eyes squinted against the smoke, holding the door open for them and then shutting it when they went inside. With Jack thinking to himself,

43

He is not going to tell me what he's going to do or when he is going to do it, and that's what he means by pain.

By three o'clock the only customers remaining were the all-night ones, and they were settled in. Jack went out the back-parlor door and across the alley to the manger, where George Gordon and Doctor sat outside in the shadows, drinking the coffee they brewed on the hot plate they kept in the manger. It was a busy night and there were all-night customers in the rooms over the manger, too; and there came down now a boy's voice, still with the adolescent crack in it, asking, "What made you want to go into a business like this?"

Jack went in and poured himself a cup of coffee and came back out to the alley dragging the old cane-bottomed chair and put it down between George Gordon and the Doctor and leaned back now sipping the coffee which he had never liked but which he drank anyway because George Gordon drank it and because he'd been told it was the best kind, with eggshells at the bottom. They sat there for a long time. After a while Jack's eyes became adjusted to the darkness and he could see better. Doctor had some sort of felt-lined leather case in his lap and there had been two old-fashioned pistols in it and he'd taken up one of the pistols and was cleaning it.

"What's that?" Jack asked.

"Dueling pistols," Doctor said. He had a cloth with a wad of cotton on the end of it and there was the faint aroma of gun oil. "Young fellow at the hotel paid me ten to clean um up. Axed me if I had ever seen any like. Hell, I have cleaned a thousand."

"It wasn't yesterday, either," George Gordon put in.

"That's the truth," Doctor said.

"Does he want to sell them?" Jack asked.

Doctor hawked and spat. "Wants to use them," he said.

"That's against the law," Jack said.

Both darkies laughed out loud.

The crickets were throbbing loudly in the tall grass along the alley. It was a hot night with not much breeze.

Now Jack lit a cigarette and began to talk. He told them about Woolworth. He took his time telling it and the Negroes listened without interrupting, two black silent wells, and he dropped the story into them as Gordon sat with his chair propped back against the wall smoking the bitter Gauloises and the Doctor leaned forward wheezing as he cleaned the dull-gleaming dueling pistols by alley light.

"It looks like he has got me," Jack concluded.

Out of the manger's open door drifted the aroma of chemicals, Jack didn't know what they were. That was the Doctor's business, as were some other things on Vinegar Hill that Jack didn't know about.

"There ain't nothing you can do," George Gordon said.

"There has got to be something," Jack said.

"You can go to Richmond," Gordon said. "Or New York City. He ain't going to bother you there."

"No," Jack said. He had already considered leaving and was not going to do it. He remembered the bindle stiffs in front of the pool hall and the dozens like them who lived in the woods on the other side of the railroad tracks and the tens of dozens of them he had seen trudging along the roads or sleeping under the bridges or dead under the bridges, for all he knew. And he told the Negroes about them.

"But you are going to be worse off than they are if you

stay around here," Gordon said.

"Hell, I belong here," Jack said.

"Now you talking 'bout something else," Gordon said.

Across the alley, in the main house, one of the girls was crying. It sounded like the twelve-year-old, but Jack was not sure. There were several of them who would cry in the night like that, sometimes to hustle money from rich students and at other times because they could not help it. Jack had learned to distinguish these kinds of crying from the kind that obliged him to step in and do his job. Of course, he knew Gordon could do it as well as he could, but you could not have a Negro doing a job like that in a whorehouse patronized by white gentlemen.

He watched Gordon now. He admired the way the Negro went on about his business when Woolworth was in there with Marguerita. He himself wanted to be hard like that, but he sensed it was something that could not be explicitly taught the way the sucker punch or the knee to the groin could be taught. The best you could do was know somebody who was truly hard like that and pick it up by osmosis. Although he'd had a lot of time to get it that way and nothing had happened yet.

"Maybe I ought to wait until he gets up," Jack said.

"That ain't going to do you no good," Gordon said.

"Maybe he will be in a better mood."

"Hunh-uh," Gordon said. "He'll be hung over. And he ain't going to change his mind anyway."

"I'd like to kill the son of a bitch," Jack said.

Doctor said, "Naw, you don't want to do that." He wheezed when he spoke.

"Like hell I don't," Jack said.

The Doctor chuckled deep in his throat. "You might think you want to," he said.

"Think, hell."

"Maybe if you was to get what you wants you would look at it different," Doctor said. "You got to be gentle in this world." He snapped open his straight razor and began to whittle on a stick of wood.

"Jack got a nailed foot," Gordon said.

"All my daddys had a nailed foot," Jack said.

Gordon said, "The first one didn't. Besides, it don't matter what your daddys did. You got to figure out what to do for your own self."

"He can't send me to jail for buying exam questions."

"Then he find some other way. That nailed foot is going to get you in trouble."

"You better listen to him," the Doctor said.

Jack didn't talk any more about it. He could never explain to Negroes what being a Cabell of Virginia meant.

"I left a place once," Gordon said. The argument had gone out of his voice and he was speaking contemplatively. "A place and a woman both."

"Are you glad you did it?" Jack asked.

"No," Gordon said. "I am sorry I did it." He tried to light a cigarette and Jack saw his hands were trembling.

"They would of killed me," Gordon said. His hands were trembling very violently now. He shook out the match and just sat there with the match's slim smoke curling up. "They killed her," he said.

Redness was radiating out over the tops of Charlottesville's low buildings as Jack Cabell came striding down off Vinegar Hill onto Main Street. At the bottom of the hill, near Aycock's, men were sleeping in doorways and huddled up against the sides of buildings. At one place they were lying out across the sidewalk, covered with newspapers. Jack had to step over them. They stank. Ahead of him, three blocks up the street, he saw his grandfather, in shirtsleeves, carrying in a bundle of newspapers that had been thrown on the sidewalk. There were more bundles on the sidewalk and when Jack got there he picked them up, carried them in, undid the baling wire, and set them in the stands. The headlines said the Japanese army had attacked the Mukden garrison over in China, killing all the defenders. There were photographs of Japanese planes carrying bombs wired to their bellies.

"I will work down here today if you want," Jack said.

His grandfather, who was arranging cigars in the case, looked up at him sharply.

"I thought you had plenty of work," he said. He was standing there looking at Jack across the counter. There was an American flag hanging on the wall behind him and his blue eyes behind the spectacles picked up the flag's blue.

"I have got to work up there," Jack said. "I have got to take anything I can get."

"Like hell you do," his grandfather said. "I would have loaned you the money."

"Then why didn't you?"

"I'd have loaned you the money and been glad to do it," the old man went on. "But there isn't any stopping you. You think it is smart to work in a nigger whorehouse. Well, it's too bad your father wasn't here to whip that out of you. Because you have got whores on the brain. Either it is the black whores on Vinegar Hill or that white whore out back. But it is always whores; you have got to have your nose stuck up the twat of some whore. Whether you call it love or money doesn't make any difference."

"You don't understand," Jack said.

"Don't hand me that," his grandfather said. "You see this?" He seized an electric fan, eight feet high on its iron

48

stand, picked it up, and held it straight out at arm's length. He held it there, his arm not moving.

"You think you can do that?" he asked.

His grandfather had challenged Jack this way before and he knew without trying that although he could pick up the fan, he could not hold his arm out straight once he'd done so.

"I understand better than you think," the old man said. He put the fan down. "Because the other parts of me work just as good as this arm does. And I am not talking about dipping your lizard. I have dipped my lizard a lot more times than you ever will. I'm talking about living with your nose up some twat. Living that way.

"Hell, when I worked for that blind man down at Crozet, the one that had the young wife, I used to take her out back of the store, out in the orchard, and do it to her up in the apple tree. But when I got done I went back to my business. What in the hell do you think you're doing, cheating at the university?"

"They haven't proved anything," Jack said.

"I'll tell you what you were doing," the old man said. "You were so busy with your nose stuck up black twat and white twat, which stinks all the same, that you didn't have time to read the books. So you thought you would pay the twat money for the cheating papers. I have got a good mind to throw you out of my house. Because it is my house. There is no point fooling around about that any more. It is my house and your father is down in Louisa with his nose stuck up a . . . No, I won't say it. I won't go that far."

"I read what's in the books," Jack said. "I catch up in the summers."

"No, you don't," the old man said. "Because when you do that you only have to live up to your own notions. You don't have to live up to anybody else's notions. That's the trouble with you. You never want to do it anybody else's way but your own."

Jack didn't say anything.

"Fix it," his grandfather said.

"Sir?"

"Fix it, whatever it takes. If it takes money I will pay the money. Fix it."

Jack went back to Vinegar Hill and tried to fix it. George Gordon and Marguerita were sitting in the kitchen having breakfast together and Jack got Gordon to drive him out to the shantytown where the girl lived. And he stood there in the doorway offering her sums of money to leave town. But the girl, who was partly crippled, had a mother lying in bed there and Jack saw the old woman through the stinking open doorway. The girl was very polite and said she understood the difficulties but was not going to leave because of the old woman and obviously could not take the old woman out of the house, let alone out of town, since the mother could not control her bladder and was dying anyway. So Jack rode back to Marguerita's with George Gordon, got off there, and walked home, thinking about what his grandfather had said. There was not much to think about. He had worked around a whorehouse long enough to know that the men who got fascinated with that stuff were never the men who worked there. They were more likely to be men like Woolworth or like his grandfather, who looked down on whores.

Jack had mixed feelings about his grandfather. He admired him for his grit and hard work, but beyond that he did not respect him. To Jack's way of thinking, the old man had watched his granddaughters growing up to be sluts, and had done nothing about it; had sat beaming at the head of the Cabell dinner table during the months when the absent Jack couldn't afford the board money, and had not cared; had owned the cash to put his son-in-law, Jack's father, into business, and had not done it; had loved not even his wife; had loved, if anything, that fifty-dollar American flag which to Jack as to any Cabell was the emblem of enemy occupation, and would carry it rootlessly around to any town that seemed suitable for a store and hang it over the cash register and be loyal to its bought cloth. Still, Jack thought, he has raw, mean blood and I have got some of it in me and it is a good thing, too. It is time the Cabells had some raw, mean blood.

4

The phone was ringing and no one answered it. Phoebe got up and ventured out into the living room. Everyone was gone. There were half-filled glasses all around and the stale stench of cigarettes. A pair of two-toned oxfords had been left on one of the sofas. The phone was still ringing. She went to the room Colette and her brother shared. The door was open and the bedcovers were on the floor and there were lipstick smears on the sheets. Pillows were on the floor, too. Still the phone was ringing. A stark, gray daylight came through the windows. She went back to the living room, picked up the phone, and said hello.

"Just don't hang up," Pat said. His voice was close, as if his lips were touching her ear again.

"Where are you?" she asked.

"Monticello Hotel."

It was chilly in the room and the morning light glowed in smudges through the half-filled glasses and there was the smell of spilled liquor coming up from the rug.

"Tell me how you want it and we will do it your way," Pat said.

"Please, just leave me alone," she said. She looked out the window toward Woolworth's now and there was no one coming up the walkway. She had hoped to see her brother out there.

"I have got to talk to you," Pat said.

"No."

"I have come three hundred and fifty miles to talk to you."

"Please, no."

"I'm coming over," he said.

She dropped the phone and ran downstairs. Bill's desk was there. She grabbed a pencil, started to write him a note, then tore it up and went outside. It was chilly and she was only wearing a summer dress, but she did not dare go back. She hurried quickly along the flagstone walkway by the mansion and up to Woolworth's front door. She rapped with the big brass knocker. There was no response. She was turning away when she saw the taxicab pulling into the driveway. She started to run around the side of the house, but saw it was Woolworth. So she came back and stood by the cab while he was paying the driver.

Woolworth emerged, adjusting his spectacles. His eyes were red and the glasses magnified them.

"Good morning, Miss Phoebe," he said. "What brings you out so bright and early?"

"I'm going for a walk," she said.

"It sure does make me mighty proud to have two pretty girls in the family now instead of just one," he said. He had told her this many times, that she was part of his family now.

"It is pretty cold to be without a sweater or something," he said. He was moving toward his front door and she followed him.

"I don't mind," she said.

"Mighty early, too."

"I like to get out early," she said. "We used to do that back home."

Woolworth opened the front door and stood there looking down at her.

"How do you like your school?" he asked.

She saw a car turning the corner from High Street. "It's just fine," she said.

"You can learn a lot of useful things at that school," he said. "You can learn to be of some use in this world."

Now the car, a Model T, rolled slowly by.

She knew now he wasn't going to ask her in, and began edging away from him. Far up First Street she saw another taxicab coming on. Pat Roosevelt was sitting up in it, driving. He was peering out at the numbers of the houses.

"It was nice talking to you," Phoebe said. She edged away more now and was standing out in the driveway.

"I would go on your walk with you, but I'm not as young as I used to be," Woolworth said. "I expect I will step inside and listen to my radio."

She was smiling and moving away and the taxicab was coming on.

"I am fifty-three years old," Woolworth said, and she felt her face smiling and turned away from him and when she heard the door close she began running around the side of the house and through the flower beds and across the alley and there was a cat that thought she was chasing it and it scampered away yowling. She ran up the back stairs of the Cabell house and knocked on the door. There was silence. She didn't hear anyone moving in the house. It was very cold in her summer dress and her breath frosted out in front of her and fogged the back door's window. From across the alley now she heard Roosevelt pounding on the front door of the Slave Quarters and, timing her knocking with his, she tried again. This time a light went on and someone came to the kitchen door. It was a maid, who was dressed in a flannel nightgown and wore a bandanna on her head.

"I'm here to see Miss Cabell," Phoebe said. She didn't remember the girl's first name.

"Ain't nobody up, miss."

"That's all right," Phoebe said. "I'll wait downstairs."

The maid led her to the living room, which was still dark. The drapes were pulled and there was a faint glow of daylight coming over the top of them. Phoebe groped and found an armchair and sat down in it.

"Don't bother to wake anybody up," she said. "I'll just wait in here."

She had been sitting in the darkened parlor for half an hour when a young man came running up the front steps, burst into the hallway, and hung his coat on the newel post. Now he peered into the living room.

"Grandmother?" he said.

"No." Now she remembered the sister's name. "I'm a friend of Dorothy's," she said.

"Were you at the A E P party?"

"No," she said. "Were you?"

"No."

"I like to get out early in the morning," Phoebe said. "I like to take walks."

Jack peered into the room but he could not see the girl, only the rectangular glow of the picture frames and her dark form in the chair his grandmother always sat in and the antimacassars on the backs of the chairs, shining.

He went back to the smoking room. He could not imagine being so easeful in life as to be able to afford taking a walk. He thought that the girl must be rich. He went to the cabinet and poured himself a tumblerful of whiskey and began to drink.

Now he heard radio music coming down from his sister's room. It was Eddie Cantor singing "Potatoes are cheaper, tomatoes are cheaper, now's the time to fall in love." Dot always played the radio in the morning. She would turn it on before she got out of bed. Her fiancé had given it to her. His father was a manufacturer of radios. Jack sat there listening to Eddie Cantor and drinking whiskey.

He'd spent two whole days in this room on the weekend Colette married Bill London. And later, drunk, had gone to the reception, cornered her in the garden, and made her promise not to let her husband "trap" her in the hotel room on their honeymoon.

He just didn't want anything to change. He'd been with her every day in the weeks leading up to her marriage. And he still had hope.

Jack had asked Colette to marry him and she'd said all right and they'd gone to Woolworth with it. Who'd said no, and who'd been angered by even being asked, since he believed that his agreement with Jack, which had been five years old at the time, covered honorable intentions as well as dishonorable ones. But he had let Jack off that time.

The next day, with Woolworth gone away for two weeks' National Guard summer camp, Jack had been sitting there with Colette on the mansion's front porch when the postman brought London's marriage proposal. She even let Jack read the letter. And the next night, after they made love out in the Slave Quarters, she told him, as she was putting her clothes back on, "I had to say yes to Bill."

Which gave Jack little time to raise money for an

elopement. She said she couldn't consider it without the money because Woolworth was sure to cut her off. A couple of days later, again on the front porch—she was wearing her red summer dress—Colette told him that her mother had put the announcement in the *Daily Progress*. And from then on, she always managed to make it sound as if the marriage was something that was being done to her, not something she herself was doing. It was all something Mama did, or Bill did. For a time Jack had believed in this interpretation. Then he hated her.

It wouldn't be right to go back on it, she said—all those people. And so the days of front-porch expostulations and telephone arguing drifted on and then the marriage took place with Jack standing drunk by the window in this room looking up the street to the gray stone spire of the Episcopal church, where it was happening.

Since then, a year ago, he had not quit looking for some way to set things straight. He had even traveled around to the county courthouses looking for Cabell wills leaving him land or money. And the only time he could get his mind off it was when he forced himself to concentrate on the law studies.

But the rest of the time, toiling in the laundry, or at Marguerita's; in class, at the pool hall, walking the mile and a half back and forth from the university, it was with him all day every day. It was the first thing he thought about in the morning and the last thing he thought about at night. And Colette was right there across the alley with Bill London, whom he despised.

Who had once been his friend, in their freshman year his best and only friend, before Jack wised up, before he came to see London as one of a climbing type that was more ubiquitous to the university than any honeysuckle vine; who comes to the university at sixteen, climbing, a type, a species as a saprophytic vine is a species; he looks for no friends, needs no friends, wants only contacts, so friendly is he. London, who had used Jack to meet Colette and who dropped him as soon as he got in with the polo set; London, who was blandly handsome like a wax manikin in a Richmond department store, and as warm; who had a soothing, deep, honeyed, and empty voice; who wasn't even a man and yet who had filled out to be muscular and broadshouldered under the expensive brown suits he bought with Jefferson Woolworth's money; who was much stronger than Colette and who had her alone to himself all night every night; who was strong enough certainly to overpower her and to Jack's way of thinking, gross enough to enjoy doing it. Jack ached with the wish to go across the alley and save her. Every night he wanted to do that. And always he was glad to see dawn. He had a rifle, too, a 30–30, and some evenings would kneel in the darkness of his attic room with the rifle propped on the window sill and sight the thing at the shadows on their bedroom shade. Always on London's shadow, and sometimes on hers. Lately he had taken to loading the gun before he did so.

There came a tapping at the door. "Jack?" It was his mother.

"Yes, ma'm."

"Are you all right?" Her voice had a teasing, sweet quality to it.

"Yes, ma'm."

"What are you doing?"

"Nothing."

"You scalawag, you come out of there," his mother said.

"In a little while."

The doorknob rattled gently.

He poured himself another tumbler of whiskey, went over to the leather ottoman, sat down on it, and began whispering urgently to the two empty chairs.

"I don't know what to do," he said. And sat there listening to the silence of the chairs.

Thinking, I would have kissed his ass, too, and been glad of it. But now I do not know what he is going to do or when he is going to do it and that's what he means by pain.

They were all in the dining room and the grandmother spoke up. "We need a man at this table," she said.

Dot leaned over and murmured to Phoebe. "It's too early in the morning for a man, if you ask me," she said.

Now Jack came into the dining room. He took the seat at the head of the table, next to Phoebe, on her right. He struck her with his sheer physical presence; she found him to be intensely handsome, powerful, startling. Then she recognized him, the young man who'd fought for her. His hand was resting on the white tablecloth close to her own. She saw on his knuckles a little caked crescent of blood. It was about half an inch above the signet ring. It was a beautiful ring, and it had the same coat of arms that was on her pocket watch. But whereas the watch's colors had faded down into pastels, the colors of the ring's crest were bright and hard. There was a row of five silver diamonds on a red shield, and surmounting the shield, the head of an elephant in colors of yellow and green. Inside the diamonds were little black dots Phoebe knew were fleurs-de-lis and underneath the shield was the scroll with the Latin words that, translated, meant "Faithful and Grateful." His hand was almost touching hers. He was looking down the table at the five Cabells and the grandmother seated there.

Jack's mother asked him to say grace.

They bowed their heads and through mostly closed eyes Phoebe saw his strong young hand near hers.

"Jack," his mother said.

There was a long silence.

"Oh, for God's sake, Jack," Dot put in. "Say it and get it over with."

"Leave him alone," the grandmother said, and recited grace herself.

"I don't know what you want him at the head of the table for when he can't say grace," Dot said.

"Hush up," his grandmother said. "Leave him alone."

Jack ate slowly and said nothing. He was acutely conscious of his family ranging along the table there. They all seemed to act as if they would always have meals like this together, they seemed to take the family for granted, and he was thinking to himself that this might be the last time he would be here with them, ever. He was drunk, of course, and it had only barely gotten through to him that the pretty girl was London's sister. Although he was clear about some other things.

For instance, he understood now why he had failed to hold the Cabell family together. It was simple and clear. It was because his grandfather, who was no Cabell, paid the bills. It was very easy to understand when he was drunk, although when he was sober it seemed more complicated. But he knew now why this room was fraught with unfinished business. And knew that the family would break up and its members die off one by one with the business still unfinished. It was money and nothing but money.

"Let's go out to Lee Park and play catch," his kid brother said.

"I can't," Jack said.

"Aw—why?"

"I have to be somewhere."

"Are you going to the football game?" his mother asked.

"No, ma'm."

"You ought to go to the football game," she said. "You work too hard."

"No harder than anybody else," he said.

"What about you, Phoebe?" Jack's mother asked. "Are you going?"

"I don't think so."

"Jack, you ought to take Phoebe to the football game," his mother said.

"I'm going to Louisa."

Dot looked up. "What for?" she asked.

"It is none of your business," Jack said.

"Well, you had better not take the car."

"Don't worry about it."

"Because Sidney and I have to use the car."

"Are you-all going to the synagogue?" Jack asked.

"Yes," Dot said.

"Dorothy," the grandmother said.

"I'm taking instructions," Dot said. "I don't see anything wrong with that."

The kid brother spoke up. "You ought to marry a Christian," he said. He hadn't eaten any breakfast and was sitting back in the chair pounding his fist into his baseball glove.

"Let her alone," Jack said.

"All I said was—"

"Don't say anything. She is your sister and you treat her with respect."

"Well, you had better not take the car," Dot said.

Jack didn't say anything.

"Just remember this isn't your house," Dot said.

Being drunk, Jack knew how things were run. It was the money. Dot knows that all the time, he thought now. She knows that even when she is sober. That is what explains Sid. The university seemed to be full of rich kikes from New York and New Jersey. They were the only ones who could afford to go there any more. They had plenty of money and did not have to work. They got good grades and participated in the university politics. There were even some of them on the Honor Council. Then, too, there was Bill London on the Honor Council. So Jack would be glad to leave the university once he had graduated from the law school. He wanted to live by his own standards. He did not like outside standards so much, not for himself, although he knew the law was nothing more than their lore. But he detested outside standards and those who made a career of imposing them.

Before long he was alone with the girl. She was sitting quietly next to him at the table. She was a shapely, graceful girl and very beautiful. His grandmother was in the stuffed chair in the front room. Jack could see her in there with the Bible on her lap, her lips moving as she read. His mother was in the kitchen. He sat there looking down the empty table and imagining all the Cabells around it with his father at the head of the table.

"I was noticing your ring," the girl said.

Dot was yelling down the stairs. "Jack! Telephone!"

He stood up. "I am obliged to go to Louisa," he said.

The girl was alone at the table.

"It's for you, Jack!" Dot screamed.

"I hear it's nice down there," Phoebe said. She was devastatingly beautiful and did not resemble her brother.

Dot was standing in the doorway. "Come get the phone or I'm going to hang up," she said.

"I'm not coming to any phone," Jack said.

The girl stood up. "I suppose I'll finish my walk," she said. She had no idea of where she could go.

"Why not drive down to Louisa with me?" Jack said.

On their way out to the car they ran into Bill London, who was coming down the alley with some curly-headed fellow Jack hadn't seen before. London didn't speak to Jack but directly to the girl.

"We're all going up to Rappahannock," he said. She got in Jack's car as if she hadn't heard him. London went around to the passenger window. "It's Daddy," he said. His coat was open and the gold fraternity pin caught the sunlight and shone out of his white shirt. The curly-headed fellow, who was stocky and well-built, stood off to one side, waiting.

"We're all going up," London said. "We have to go now." He didn't look at Jack.

Now Colette came through the garden gate and out into the alley. She was wearing a white tennis outfit with a white peaked hat. Jack could not see her eyes under the eyeshade there.

London stood back a little from the car. "Aren't you going to get out?" he said.

But Phoebe just sat there looking straight ahead. "What's wrong with Daddy?" she said.

"We have got to take him to the hospital."

"What's wrong with him?" she asked again.

"It is the same thing," Bill London said.

Jack saw that the girl was blushing and he had a feeling that it had something to do with the curly-headed fellow.

London reached out his hand toward the car door and was opening it when Jack spoke.

"That belongs to my family," he said.

London stood with his hand on the door looking at Jack

and not moving. Jack had not raised his voice. Nobody said anything. London let his hand slide off the door.

"She has got to go with us," he said.

Colette was standing by the garden gate.

"Why don't you open the door, then?" Jack said.

"No," London said. "It is your property, like you say."

"I will give you one minute to open it," Jack said. Nobody moved.

So this is it, Jack thought. You don't like it very much when it is on the other foot, do you, you son of a bitch? London's wide, handsome mouth looked weak and unsettled, as if he didn't know what to do with it.

"Come on, Phoebe," London said. But the door didn't open. Jack went around to the driver's side and got in. As he drove away down the alley, Bill, Colette, and Pat Roosevelt were standing where they'd been for the last minute.

When she saw the signet ring on his hand, and made the connection between that and the coat of arms on the watch's face, she decided to marry him. She took the ring to be a secret signal to her deepest self. He was a Cabell of Virginia and he had fought for her. In a way, he was what she had expected all along. It was almost as if she'd made him up.

Besides, he was handsome, and she liked that. She thought he had a face like the poet Lord Byron. Or that he must resemble the Gray Ghost, Mosby. She had never seen a picture of either of those men (though she had known Mosby when he was old), but she was sure of the resemblance. Honor outside, honor inside.

So Cabell would save her, and she was confident about getting her way with him. She had used her beauty for years now to get what she wanted; which hadn't been so very much: refuge, mainly.

Now, here with Jack in the Model A, moving through bright yellows and reds toward Louisa, she had it turned on all the way. She was doing it the way she always did.

She would sense the man's physical presence, listen feelingly to his tone of voice, move with his moods as they shifted; tuning herself in to him as if he were a radio station. She had done this many times and it usually did not take long for the young man to lose his voice, if he'd been talking, or to start talking if he'd been quiet. She knew how to move men, and this was her great secret.

She talked about his family. She had read a book on the Cabells of Virginia and knew most of the main branches and where the old plantations were. She talked to him about that. She was confident. She did not care about whether he had any money or whether he was seeing any other girl. If there was a rival, the girl would have to give way before her, as rivals always had. If he lacked money now, he would make it later on because he had honor. She was as sure of that as she was of the notion that he looked like Lord Byron and Mosby. Honor drew money to itself if you were a man and it made you beautiful if you were a woman. She was glad she understood the fundamental, practical things like that because she knew her position was precarious and called for practicality.

She liked the elegant clean simplicity of Jack's suit and the quality of the silence that came off him. She fancied herself a great listener to silences. Here, she believed, was a man who would speak only when he had something to say and who would never use his mouth in a dishonorable way.

(That had been part of the final hell delusions in New York: the vision of mouths talking, greasy know-it-all persuading mouths talking, until finally her eyes' attention had gone only to the mouths and she'd not seen faces any more, only mouths. She had gone through three weeks' horror staring at mouths and looking for a quiet one or an honest one, but they were greasy mouths persuading and at last the hospital attendants had been obliged to lash her arms in front of her with a belt to keep her from clawing her face any more and they had put her head in a vise to keep her from sinking her teeth into her shoulders. She had ridden that way three hundred miles from New York City to Rappahannock, Virginia, with her father, who'd rented the ambulance, sitting beside her stroking her forehead and telling her it would be all right. And that he would be damned if he ever let her go up North again. Which she'd done in the first place because her one-time piano teacher, Jessica Ross, the Jewess, had gone to Barnard and Phoebe wanted to be like her; Jessica Ross, who had killed herself with a shotgun for love of Old Man Jim; although Phoebe did not know that part of it yet.)

Later on, she told herself, she would learn what there was to know about Jack, the details, but they didn't matter now. He was sad and had suffered, she thought, because he had not found the woman who could match his emotional depth and intense honor. But she would take care of that and he would take care of her. Life could begin.

This is my last chance, Jack thought. I have got to see him and he has got to help me. If he can't help me he has got to advise me. The Negroes don't know what to do this time.

They were driving along through tall pines and oaks and linden trees. There were a few dark-green leaves left, but it was mostly bright yellows, reds. Now they broke out of the trees to where the open, rolling fields were and there were thick power lines strung out, coming from nowhere and going nowhere. Herefords were grazing under the power lines in the ancient rocky fields. They were coming down the hill to the South Anna River and Jack pulled the car off to the side at a place where fishermen parked. He didn't know Pat Roosevelt was following him.

He saw that Phoebe was wearing a short-sleeved summer dress, and he took off his coat and put it around her shoulders. Her hair smelled the way Colette's hair used to smell. Now he got a good look at her. This London girl excited him. She had beautiful breasts and he looked at her in profile, the graceful slope of nose, long black lashes, chatoyant eyes somewhere between deep blue and violet. Jack wished he had time for her. She would be a good piece for her own sake and it would be some good revenge on Bill London. But there wasn't time for anything now. No time.

"Your grandfather's place was near here, wasn't it?" she asked. She was referring to his paternal grandfather, Frederick Price Cabell, of the true blood.

It was quiet in the car and the wind whispered in the windows. Down below them the water licked at the bridge. A slick black boulder was humped out of the middle of the river.

"That's Coecacoeroe's Rock," Jack said. This was the first time it had been above water in his lifetime, although he had known for years where it was, and what color it was. The drought was in its second year; crops were scorched in the fields and the foxes were rabid.

"Who is that?" Phoebe asked.

"She was queen of the Pamunkey Indians. She brought the Pamunkeys over to the British side. But she ran away during Bacon's Rebellion to be with the other Indians. They captured her out there on that rock."

It was quiet now except for the water's lapping.

They had captured Jack's great-great-great-great-great-great grandfather, Cornelius Cabell, out there, too, on that rock. He had been the king's representative to the

Pamunkeys. When his wife died he had taken up with the Indian queen. He had gone out to fetch her back when she fled. He was the man who translated her apology into English—the one she spoke for the king of England (or that he made up)—and included with it in the letter, his own apology. That had been in a drought year, also; the foxes had been rabid then, too, and the wolves.

On the other side of the river this drought had trapped fish in isolated stagnant pools which had dried up entirely or were fast drying up. Their dead white bellies shone in the fall sun. High above the power lines, buzzards were circling down.

Now a banner-whipping carful of revelers came plummeting down the far hill, horn blaring, crossed the bridge, speeding toward them to the thunk of boards, and sped on past. In the intervals between horn blasts Jack could hear the car radio. It was playing the news, more about the Japanese. Then the car disappeared over the top of the hill and there was quiet once more, whisper of wind, lap of water.

"What are those little white things over there?" she asked.

"I don't know."

"It's beautiful here," she said. "It's so still."

"Yes."

"I suppose you feel at home here."

"All this belongs to a dentist now," he said.

"But I'll bet you like to come here and imagine it's still in the family."

This was true.

"If this were my family's place, I know I would do that," she said.

He started up the car. She was smiling at him. She had a pretty smile.

"One day you'll get this back," she said. "When you're a famous judge."

"I don't want to be a judge," he said.

"A district attorney, then."

"No," he said. "Especially not that. Lawyer for the defense. That is what I want to be."

Nearing Louisa, they came over the top of a hill and saw two cars blocking the road. There were young men standing by the cars. Jack braked and came to a stop in front of them. They were university students, stopping traffic and offering passers-by free drinks out of paper cups. Coming up to both windows, they looked in and offered cups.

"It's the fellow who works at Marguerita's," one of them said.

"You-all had better get to the game," Jack said. Someone dragged back the youth who'd recognized him and was telling him to shut up.

Jack had a drink with the students, then drove around the cars and proceeded on toward Louisa.

"Will you have this?" Phoebe asked.

"Don't you drink?"

"No."

"Well, you are in the wrong place, coming to Charlottesville," he said.

"I hope not," she said. "I hope I'm not in the wrong place."

Louisa was a county seat with an old red brick courthouse surrounded by big trees and shops on the square. As they pulled into town, Phoebe was talking about the slaves. She had a theory that the colored people had been better off as slaves than they were now.

"After all," she said, "they were looked after. They had a place to go."

It was chilly in the car and Jack took her to sit on one of the benches in the square, out in the sun. The bench faced the Katz Clothing Store and Jack could see his father in there.

Warlock Cabell, a tall, heavy, whitehaired man, was bent down on one knee, measuring a farmer's inseam. He was meticulous in this work, as in everything. He took his time. He would insert the rubber piece into the man's crotch, adjust it, then take it out and insert it again. Finally he got it set to his satisfaction and carried the tape down to where the cuff would be and made a mark there with a little sliver of soap.

On the courthouse lawn near Jack and Phoebe were some tourists; a man and a woman and five children. The man had a camera slung around his neck and was taking photographs of the Confederate memorial statue. The local people, mostly farmers, it seemed, were across the street on the sidewalk in front of the shops, standing near the automobiles, talking. They did not look in the windows of the shops.

Seated nearby on the curb, on the courthouse side, was an old, dark Negro in brand-new overalls and a faded denim shirt. Next to him was hitched a horse and wagon. A large, heavy horse, it stood there stolidly. The wagon was made all of wood, except for the metal hoops around the wheels. There was hay in the wagon and wisps of it stuck out over the top and through the apertures in the sides. Now the tourist, who wore a baseball cap with the legend *New York Yankees*, went up behind the Negro and began snapping pictures. He put himself at an angle where he could get the Negro and the horse in the same picture. When he motioned to the children they came and lined up along the curb between the horse and the Negro. The man tried to get the woman into the picture, but she wouldn't come. She stood behind him and watched as he snapped the pictures.

"So you went to school in New York City," Jack said. He was watching his father. The old man was still measuring the inseam and Jack thought to himself, I couldn't do it. I couldn't do it. That is not what they meant by faithful and grateful.

"Yes," Phoebe said.

"What's it like?"

"It seemed to me everybody was cruel," she said. "In the city."

"You don't find it like that down here."

"Oh, no," she said. "This is home."

Jack was sober now, but he still wasn't paying much attention to the girl. He was remembering the last time he had come down to Louisa. He had been looking for a lost legacy, hoping to save Colette and himself. After that he had gone to more than a half dozen other courthouses. He had found many of the old pieces of paper, dry and brittle now, with the inked signatures of eight generations of his fathers on them, but no legacy. The papers in the Louisa courthouse showed his father selling off his grandfather's plantation bit by bit in the years between 1893 and 1916. It seemed to Jack that he must have sold all of it by now, although he couldn't be sure. He had kept on hoping there might be something left, even one acre. He believed that if he had only one acre he could make it.

Now he watched as his father finished with the customer and climbed the steps to where Katz sat perched high above the shop floor in an office that was more like a pulpit, and about as small. Jack had been into Katz's to meet his father at the close of the working day and had

72

heard the proprietor preaching business from there. Katz was a short fellow and the partition around the office was high. So that when he was sitting down and Warlock Cabell had to ask him for permission to go to lunch, it was necessary to climb the stairs. The rest of the time, the most one saw of him was the tip of his eyeshade gliding back and forth above the partition like a green tongue licking translucent lips. Now Jack's father came down the steps and out onto the sidewalk.

"There's my father," Jack said.

"That big man?"

"Yes."

"That's the most distinguished-looking man I've ever seen in my life," Phoebe said.

Jack had heard other people say this, that his father was distinguished-looking, but it wasn't until he had been at the university for several years that he learned that there were men in the world who were called distinguished without the "looking" part tacked on. He discovered that law school deans and apple-growing politicians and brain surgeons were distinguished and that all rich men were distinguished, too. Since then it had pained him to hear his father referred to as distinguished-looking.

A woman had approached his father and Warlock Cabell doffed his hat and stood there beaming down at her. He was a beautiful, strong-looking man with healthy-looking ruddy skin and a graceful broadshouldered physique. He had a good-sized belly on him but it was covered up by the vest of his elegant suit and he carried it well. He looked like the president of a railroad.

The woman had asked his father the time of day. Jack had seen this ritual many times and stood back now, watching. It was like the Catholic mass; it always went the same way.

"The time of day?" There followed a long pause, as the big, handsome man seemed to ponder on how such a thing might be found out. Then a look of happy remembrance would cross his face, as if he'd just recalled that, by an unusual and fortunate circumstance, he himself happened to be carrying a timepiece. Deftly, gracefully, he fished in his vest pocket for the watch, and brought it out glittering into the sunlight, an elegant, gold-filigreed one at the end of a gold chain. Positioning the watch in a well-manicured hand, he thumbed the button and the cover flipped up. Carefully, he studied the watch's face, as if what he saw there could be interpreted in several different ways. Then, amused by what he saw, but tentative in his conclusion, he ventured to tell the woman the time of day. Then he looked once more, as if verifying that it was indeed good old twelve-fifteen; although if it was, the question had first been posed at twelve-twelve. Finally, with a flourish, he snapped the thing shut and returned it to his vest pocket. He told the time beautifully, and Jack had long suspected that persons who stopped his father to ask the hour did not want that so much as they wanted to be gentled down out of the new, faster wrist-watch time they themselves were obliged to run on.

Because Warlock Cabell was never in a hurry about anything. He ran on Old Time. That was the best thing about him, Jack thought. He was a distinguished time-teller and Jack loved him for that. And wished that time-telling paid something so that his father would not be obliged to spend his life down on one knee whiffing farmer balls.

"Where is your coat?" his father asked him.

"Back there with the girl." He had left Phoebe sitting on the bench in front of the courthouse.

74

"You are going to catch cold," his father said. They were walking down the street together.

The hotel was an old red brick place, two stories high, a century and a half old, with a long white railing out front, a long wooden porch with chairs and swings on it. It was beginning to get a little warmer now. The woman was sitting on the porch. This was Mrs. Rovin, who was known in Louisa as "Mr. Cabell's friend." She was a quiet, attractive brunette of fifty or so. She'd had the adjoining room to Warlock Cabell's for more than a dozen years. Jack's father doffed his hat to her as they passed and murmured good day. Now Jack followed him up to his room, where his father took a coat out of the closet and handed it to him.

"This is too big," Jack said.

"Put it on."

Jack did as he was told. He wished that they could just stay here and talk. He liked his father's room. It smelled of that same sort of lotion barbers put on your neck after they gave you a haircut. Jack always liked the smell of his father's room and the quiet sense of order here. Now he followed the big man out into the hall and down to the restaurant. Mrs. Rovin had come into the restaurant and was sitting at a table in the corner, watching them.

The darky came up and took their order and then Jack was alone with his father.

"I thought maybe I could give you a lift back home," Jack said.

His father looked at him as if he were drunk. There was something about Jack that seemed to amuse him, but he had never told Jack what it was.

"I don't need any lift," he said. His eyes were green, as Jack's were, and they looked out now from under black brows.

75

"I just thought maybe you would want to be there this weekend," Jack said.

"I have got business down here," Warlock Cabell said. "And it would seem to me you have got business up there."

"What is that?" Jack asked.

"School business."

"Yes, sir."

When the meal came, Warlock Cabell devoted his full attention to it. He was a slow eater and he seemed to consider each thing before he ate it. He loved food, and spent time with each morsel. When the meal was over, he took out a small pocketknife and began to peel the apple the darky left by his plate.

"Elegant," he said. "Elegant."

That was one of Warlock's favorite words. Jack had heard it many times, always at meals. It was only after he was in the university that he'd heard the word used in connection with anything but food.

"Elegant," his father repeated. He finished peeling the apple, quartered it, and handed one of the sections across the table to Jack.

When they went out on the front porch, the woman followed them and sat in the swing nearby. She always followed them like this.

They were alone at the end of the porch, the three of them.

"You have got to help me," Jack said.

His father sat gazing out at the slow street, belly protuberant. "How much?" he said.

"Jefferson Woolworth is trying to get me expelled from the university. If he gets the goods on me they will give me twenty-four hours to leave school."

"That ought to be long enough," his father said.

From behind them now the woman spoke up. "Young man," she said, "you are violating this place."

It was the first time Jack had ever heard her speak. It was as if the hotel itself had spoken.

"It is evil for you to bring the sins of that place down here," the woman said.

"Be quiet," his father said.

"I don't mind his coming down here," the woman said. "But I will not have him violating this place."

"Go upstairs," Warlock told her.

After a long silence, the woman arose and left. Presently Jack's father stood up and followed her. Jack was left alone in his rocking chair, looking out at the street.

He did not like the woman, but thought he knew what she meant by "violating this place." It was quiet here on the old porch and it seemed to be a place where troubles ought never to be allowed. For a hundred and fifty years men like his father had been sitting out here, behind this rail, insulated from all quickness and strife. Old Time ran here. It was not like the front porch in Charlottesville, where importunate Jews from New Jersey made love to his sisters.

Moving down the street now, passing in front of the porch, came a yellow and black Charlottesville taxicab. Jack saw Colette riding in the front seat. The curly-headed fellow was driving and Bill London was sitting in back. Jack watched the cab roll by.

His father returned and sat in the chair beside him.

"What is it?" he said.

"I bought the examinations from the niece of the night maid up at the school. Woolworth found out about it. He has the police out trying to catch the girl who sold me the examinations."

"You cheated," his father said.

"Yes."

"I thought I told you never to cheat and never to tell a lie. Even if it hurts you, never to cheat or tell a lie."

"Well, it would have hurt me pretty bad," Jack said.

"Circumstances don't matter," the old man said. "A gentleman never cheats and never tells a lie."

Jack didn't say anything.

"You will have to get a job," his father said.

"And leave school?"

"No," his father said. "You don't have to do that. They will take care of that for you."

"Couldn't you come back and talk to Woolworth?"

"What for?" the old man said. "I am not going to ask him for anything and I don't want you asking him for anything. You have got to stand up and take your medicine. I want you to be able to look any man in the world in the eye and tell him to go to hell."

"I would rather finish school first," Jack said.

"You aren't going to finish any school," his father said. "You have got to get a job."

Jack shook his head.

"Then I will give you some good advice," his father said. "If a fellow is walking down the sidewalk and steps in shit, he will go off on the grass and wipe his shoe off. Then he will go on about his business and watch where he is stepping."

Warlock Cabell stood up. He was a distinguished-looking man in a beautiful suit.

"I don't understand what that has got to do with it," Jack said.

"Well, that is all I have got to tell you."

Maybe that is all you know, Jack thought. He was experiencing a kind of deep panic he'd not known before.

Meanwhile Phoebe, who had been puzzled by being

left alone on the courthouse bench, had gotten annoyed, then angry, as Jack didn't return, and as the day got warm and then hot. She was not going to put up with being treated like that. So he wants to make sure about me, she thought. So he wants to see what I'm made of.

Thus she was glad when the taxicab rolled up. She didn't even mind Pat Roosevelt so long as her brother was there, and would have been willing to put up with him anyway for the sake of playing the game with Jack Cabell. She was good at playing the game. Let him follow me, she thought. Let him do the waiting now. And she climbed in the front seat of the taxicab, taking the place of Colette, who got out.

"Where are you going?" Bill asked Colette.

"To put an end to it," Colette said.

Phoebe didn't know what Colette was going to put an end to. It was puzzling.

"I'll come with you," Bill said.

"No," his wife said.

"But when will I see you?"

"Later," Colette said. "Back home. I have really got to put an end to it." And she walked quickly away.

"Let's find Cabell and give him his coat back," Bill said.

Phoebe had forgotten about that. She had the coat over her arm. Now the taxicab began to circle the square. There was no water coming out of the memorial fountain. The fountain was dry that year.

6

Colette Woolworth stood there under the Confederate memorial, tanned and full-figured in her white tennis outfit, waiting for Jack Cabell and watching the yellow taxicab circling the green square. She had healthy, clean-looking eyes. The whites of her eyes were very clear. She played a lot of tennis. Presently Cabell came walking down the street. The taxi glided up beside him and Pat handed Cabell his coat balled up without even stopping the car. And drove off leaving Cabell standing foolishly at the curb, holding the coat and looking down the street to where the vehicle was disappearing behind a hay wagon.

Lately Jack had begun to seem more and more helpless to Colette. And whereas this might have put off a poorer girl, who needed to be supported, it actually endeared him to her, who needed nothing at all that came in dollars. She wished she could do something for him, but could not imagine what that would be. She felt sorry for him. Everybody else seemed to be going somewhere, even if it was just plain old going to hell with liquor, but Jack, more and more, seemed like someone waiting around where he was not wanted or needed. So that the way she saw him now, standing there with the balled-up coat in his hand, looking after the vanished taxicab, was close to the way she saw him all the time.

He was always hanging around waiting for something that had already gone on and left him. Indeed, she'd be glad when he left Charlottesville, where there wasn't anything for him and wasn't going to be. Of course, it might not have been so bad if he'd just had sense enough not to enroll in the university. If it weren't for that, she believed, Jack would have had his own filling station by now or be manager of the pool hall. But he had gone anyway, and it had ruined him for those things. By breaking with him, she thought she'd be doing him a favor, removing what she believed to be the chief cause of his wanting to hang around.

But it wasn't just altruism; she was afraid of the violence in him. Besides, he seemed childish. At first he had been the mature one, and had introduced her to many new things, including sex. Especially sex. But that had been more than a decade ago, and since then she had surpassed him, so that she was the mature one now, she believed.

Colette had been to Europe eight times, had read widely and met many interesting people. She had learned how to read people, too, and to get along with them, and was as comfortable at a Negro bootleg roadhouse as she was at an ambassador's ball. She had been psychoanalyzed, she had earned a master's degree in art history from Sweet Briar, and might have gone on for a doctorate, too, if the University of Virginia had admitted women. So she was permanently more sophisticated now than Cabell, she believed. Besides, most of the young women in her set had had a romantic and sexual experience with some boy from a lower station in life, but that was something you gave up like you gave up braces and she was only sorry she'd not done it before.

The scene in the alley that morning had decided it. She knew that the threat to her husband had been serious and had nothing to do with Cabell family property. She knew there was no Cabell family property unless you counted the two remaining plots in the gray-tongued old family graveyard near Coecacoeroe's Rock, where Jack had always said they'd be buried together someday.

That was the only real estate he'd ever offered her. Of course, Colette wasn't especially interested in more real estate, since she had several million dollars' worth of it already; an entire city block of office buildings in downtown Richmond, and tens of thousands of acres of lush farmland. Indeed, when she thought about it, she supposed she was rich, although she almost never did. Only vulgar persons thought about money.

Now Jack saw her and came over to where she was.

"Where are they headed?" he asked.

She told him, and a few moments later she was in the front seat beside him as he drove rapidly up state route 522 toward Rappahannock, which was seventy or eighty miles away up in the Blue Ridge Mountains. Cabell's face was fishbelly white.

"I don't see why you won't take me back to Charlottesville," she said.

"Listen," he told her. "It is not my responsibility to take you anywhere."

"At least you could be a gentleman," she said.

"No," he said. "I am tired of being a gentleman."

He made her nervous and she decided that she'd wait until they were safely in Rappahannock before she told him. There was really too much violence in him, and besides, he would want an explanation. But how can you explain when you're wiser than someone else? she thought to herself. The way the world worked was that you could understand everybody dumber but that everybody smarter was opaque and same-seeming. So you could not understand them. And he cannot understand me, she thought. Besides, the truth would kill him. Because he still loves what I was at fourteen. It would either kill him or he would kill me if he knew who I am now.

Colette, shortly after marrying Bill London, had decided she loved sex for its own sake and would do what she liked. After all, there was nothing to deter her. If her husband did not like it, then she would get another husband. Many of the girls in her set already had. It was even considered chic. With several men and women who were willing to teach her, Colette had begun to explore.

She was fond of small, prolonged orgies. That certain bunch of well-off Charlottesvillians who had initiated her into them said that the orgies were a kind of secret tradition that had been begun by Thomas Jefferson. And Colette believed this. It seemed an exciting, civilized practice, the sort of thing Jefferson would like.

To her delight, her husband, after a little instruction, had acquiesced to the special parties and even participated in them. Thus there was a lightsome, casual mood to Colette's life these days, which she found more congenial than the tragic intensity Jack Cabell brought to everything. There were doors, everywhere, in what he looked upon as walls.

She loved to watch people's faces as they did it and to watch what they were doing and talk to them while they were doing it. She loved new partners and new combinations, slow dalliance for hours. And it pleased her sense of humorous intrigue that no one outside of the dozen regular participants seemed to have any notion of what was going on.

Once she'd sought to do Jack a favor by getting him interested. That had been half a year ago. She began by telling him about things she'd read in certain French books, and by speculating on what orgies might be like. It took him a long time to understand what she was talking about, and once he did, he dismissed it.

"I don't respect people like that," he said.

"Why not?" she asked.

"It isn't even worth talking about," he said.

But she kept at it. That's what all the summer visits to his attic were about. She would tell him her "daydreams," which were really her experiences. She would tell him at what she thought were appropriate times.

"I can't see anything wrong with it," she'd say. Then she did something he enjoyed very much and, pausing in the middle of it, looked up and said, "Can you?"

She asked him this so many times that she got him thinking about it, and one evening when she looked up and said that, he got out of bed and went over and sat down at his low-lit table where the lawbooks were.

"Listen," he said. "That stuff is no good."

"Why?"

"Because it violates you."

"I can't see how it violates you if you want to do it," she said.

"Because it lets people penetrate you."

She pulled the covers over her and turned on her back with her head on his pillow, looking up at where his naked body shone in the low golden light. His head was in deep shadow.

"And what is wrong with a little penetration?" she said.

"I am not talking about that kind."

"You mean like when somebody gets beaten up?"

"Yes," he said.

"Of course," she said. "I understand it all now. You have to be some kind of criminal if you don't want to be . . . violated."

Jack had not answered that one. Actually, he'd seen a lot of truth in the remark and had been thinking about it ever since. Shortly thereafter, Colette had discontinued her visits to the attic.

Now, three miles ahead of them up the road, was a small moving speck which Jack took to be the taxicab, and he accelerated toward it.

Colette noticed this, and thought to herself, He has always wanted to rescue somebody. The only trouble is that I do not want to be rescued.

"Phoebe doesn't know what to do about that boy," she said. "He kept calling her from New York. She used to go out with him when she was up there. I don't think she knew what he was then."

She glanced over at Cabell, who didn't say anything. Beyond him she saw the Blue Ridge Mountains, way off, and white thunderclouds rising up over them.

"Actually, I think it's just a lot of silly prejudice," she said. "Some of Daddy's best friends are Jews."

Cabell drove along silently. It was very hot in the car. The dot was resolving itself into a pickup truck, but still he drove on swiftly.

"I can understand why she's afraid of him," Colette said. "He's a college wrestling champion, or something."

Jack remained quiet.

"But I wouldn't worry about it," she said. "If he was going to beat you up he'd probably have already done so." She felt the car picking up speed and smiled within herself.

"Did you hear about my jumper?" she said.

"No."

"He was bitten by a fox."

"Where is there a telephone?" Jack asked.

Bill London had been upset by the scene in the alley that morning, but not humiliated. He was over it now and did not reproach himself for refusing to mix it up with Cabell. That was kid stuff, and besides, he knew what Cabell was and so there was no point. And he consoled himself for not fighting by the reflection that there were other ways of being brave. For instance, given the London family circumstances, he believed that marrying Colette Woolworth had been brave, and that studying three or four hours a day more than he needed to was brave. Bill London was third in his class at architecture school, and had a sufficiency of self-respect. He thought of himself as a modern man and a realist, and was not downcast by having refused to mix it up with a thug.

Now he rode along in the back seat of the taxicab, watching the hot, cloud-hung dun countryside with its tall pine trees sliding by. He had his eye on Phoebe and Pat Roosevelt, and was trying to gain some sense of how they were getting along. It was important to him that they get along well because he wanted her out of his house, and, after talking to Roosevelt this morning, believed that the New Yorker was about as good a match as she was likely to get.

He felt it was his job to impress that on her, because he had to look after all the London family. At least he told himself that, and tended to justify his actions that way. For almost ten years he'd been convinced that his father was going crazy and that he, Bill, would be called on at any minute to look after everyone. Thus he had married into the Woolworth family, he believed, out of a sense of filial responsibility. And it wouldn't be long before he would have enough money to take care of everybody, although, of course, in the meantime he did not feel obliged to have any Londons living with him.

So it was time Phoebe got married. She was in the way at the Slave Quarters and Colette did not want her there and any night she might see too much. Bill found it awkward trying to look after her and avoid her at the same time, while keeping up with studies and meeting the social responsibilities that came from being part of the Woolworth family. Then, too, there was the Honor Council. That consumed a lot of his time. He took his position on it very seriously.

Roosevelt and Phoebe had not been talking and now Bill leaned forward and said, "Why not stop at that little store up there and get us a Coke?" He fished in his pocket, took out a twenty-five-cent piece, and handed it to Phoebe.

Roosevelt pulled the car into the store's driveway, under the protruding roof, stopped next to the gasoline pump, and went inside.

"That's a good-looking boy," Bill said.

Phoebe tried to give back the twenty-five-cent piece.

"No," Bill said, "I want you to have that." He was fond of giving her little pieces of money and patting her on the back in a friendly way. He liked his sister and hoped she was unaware of what went on at the special parties. He did not want her to get the wrong notion, and wished he could explain to her what a swell friend Colette was and how he had gone after her in the first place so as to be able to take care of all the Londons when Old Man Jim finally went mad. But he was afraid she might misunderstand that, too, and so he resolved that he would show her what it was all about when he went into business with Jefferson Woolworth. He would give her everything she wanted then and would find things she'd never known enough to want and give her those, too. And he would do the same for his mother and kid brother.

"What's wrong with Daddy?" Phoebe asked.

"I don't know."

"Is he going to be all right?"

Bill shook his head. "I doubt it," he said. "You know, he is not ever going to be really right any more. That is one of the reasons I am so worried about you."

Out in the parking lot, big, infrequent raindrops were hitting down softly into the thick dust, globbing themselves blackly out of sight.

"This here Roosevelt is a right nice young fellow," Bill said. "You are not going to meet many as nice as him."

"I know," Phoebe said. She had forgotten how handsome Pat was and how gentle he could be. He seemed to have given up the intense, didactic talking that had been her chief objection to him before. All that seemed to have gone out of him.

"I don't mean to meddle in your business," Bill said.

"It's just that I never could live up North."

"I wouldn't be surprised if he had other plans now."

"What other plans?"

"That's between you and him," Bill said. "I would listen to him if I were you."

Now the rain came down heavily and they could hear it pounding on the store's tin roof. Pat was still inside.

"I think you have got to judge a fellow on his own merits," Bill said. "And not on where he comes from."

"I'll think it over," she said.

"Let me tell you," Bill said, with a vehemence that surprised him. "There are a lot of things that go on in the

88

South, too, that would surprise you."

Colette's visits to Jack's attic still troubled him. This added to his hatred of Cabell, which was already intense. London despised his former friend and felt very bad when his wife went to that attic. It was not like the special parties, when everyone was there and he knew what was going on and could watch. Those were friendly. But Bill was tortured by the attic visits and hoped they had truly stopped.

"There are a lot of things to be said for marriage," he told Phoebe. The heavy rain was roaring on the tin roof. "There is nothing like a good home," he said.

7

Pat Roosevelt was trapped deep in the country store, loving it with a scholar's love, a convert's love. He stood there at the dark wooden counter reading the label on a cylindrical tin of Red Rooster snuff.

"You want some gas?" the proprietor said.

"Sure," Pat said.

Then he was alone. It was a beautiful room, long and dim, with full-stocked shelves running along the sides and up to the ceiling. The wood floor was bare, slippery, well-worn. There was a black potbellied stove in the middle of the floor and strips of flypaper hung down from the ceiling like the tree snakes in the stories of Chateaubriand. Sacks of chicken feed were arrayed in front of the wooden counter, resting up against it. The place stank of chicken feed and Pat loved the smell. Behind the counter, tacked up on the wall, was a faded Confederate flag which Pat took to be authentic. Next to it was a photograph of Woodrow Wilson. A radio was playing. It was some sort of religious revival program. There were straw hats strung on a wire running down the length of the rainbeaten store and fishing poles stood in a stone crock over in the corner. Pat loved all this, loved the South. Which was why he'd chosen to become a Southern historian.

He'd met Phoebe while writing a paper on John Singleton Mosby, and it was through a letter she wrote that he'd gotten to meet Mosby's family over in Warrenton. Phoebe remembered Mosby, too. He had come to her birthday party when she turned five.

Now Pat was writing his doctoral dissertation on "The Chivalric Code of the Old South," and in the year and a half since Phoebe had been taken away from New York he'd had a lot of time to think about how different things were down here from the way they were up there. He had been much too rough on her before, he believed. He should have appreciated her for what she was without trying to speed up her education, he thought, and regretted having forced the doses of Darwin, Marx, and Freud on her. It had been innocent on his part, because he'd just been trying to make her know the world he came from as well as he thought he knew the world she came from. But it had been too much, he'd come to believe, and he was determined not to make that mistake again. That was the way to live to a ripe old age, his father had told him: to learn from your mistakes. Pat, a gentle fellow, had taken this to heart and tried to learn from all of his.

His new plans were to take her down to the family plantation in South Carolina. He'd recently been informed of his appointment as an assistant professor in the History Department at the University of South Carolina. He would go down there with Phoebe and teach the Southerners about themselves.

Out in the car, Bill was giving Phoebe some advice. "I am one of Jack Cabell's best friends," he said. "So I can tell you this. You had better stay away from him."

Phoebe, who had no intention of staying away from him, said nothing.

"He works at Marguerita's," Bill said.

The rain was very loud on the roof now and the driveway was turning to mud.

"Is that a restaurant?" she shouted.

"It's a whorehouse," London shouted.

This excited Phoebe, and confirmed what she already believed, that Jack Cabell was like the poet Lord Byron. He is dissolute because he is sad, she thought. But I will make him happy.

"He's cheated on his examinations in school, too," London shouted.

Just then Roosevelt opened the door and beckoned them to get out. He had three straw hats, one on his head and two in his hands. Now he went around to the taxi's trunk and brought out a camera, and after showing the store's proprietor how to work the thing, he came to stand close by Bill and Phoebe, grinning widely. He had a handsome, sunny grin.

"Nothing doing," Bill said. "Only niggers wear these."

But Pat, who was good at getting his way, got it.

So they stood there, three young people posed in a row, under the roof of a gas station in a thunderstorm, having their picture taken by the proprietor. And with Pat calculating to himself as it was being snapped where he would hang it if it turned out okay. He was a gifted photographer and had many fine photographs. One of the best of them was a frontal view of his father's South Carolina mansion (now his, Roosevelt's, deeded over), which had been enlarged to four by five feet, framed, and hung over the bed in his New York apartment. That photograph was one of the first things that had impressed Phoebe about him. It had seemed to be a mansion of great honor.

"Listen," Pat told Phoebe as they were driving off, "we don't ever have to live in New York again. I've got a place you're going to like better, a surprise." And he talked on urgently as the car moved slowly through the downpour.

Phoebe was thinking of only one thing: what her brother had told her about Jack's having cheated on the examinations. That was not like Lord Byron, nor was it anything she could excuse.

She turned around to ask Bill if he was sure about the cheating, but he had fallen asleep with his straw hat tilted down over his eyes. He had been an active lover the night before.

"Let's stop somewhere and talk about it," Pat said.

It was raining heavily. Jack saw the store and pulled in under its protruding roof. He was frightened.

"I'm sick of cars," Colette said. She got out and stood there under the roof, looking at the thunderstorm. "Sometimes it seems that only cars are solid," she said. "That it's the houses that move. I feel like I've spent my whole life in a car."

There is nobody going to help me now and I have got to do it, Jack thought. He went in to the man behind the counter, got his grandmother's fifty-cent piece broken down into change, and walked back to where the pay phone was.

The radio, which was up on the shelf by the Woodrow Wilson photograph, was playing loudly. A preacher was talking about the Storm of Fire. The world was going to be destroyed in a Storm of Fire, he said. There was much wickedness in the world.

"Turn that down, will you?" Jack yelled. The man used the oatmeal grabber and manipulated the dial with the hook.

Jack got the long-distance operator and gave her the number. The phone was slick from the perspiration of his hand. Woolworth came on the line.

"Hello?"

"This is Jack." His voice trembled when he spoke.

"Jack who?"

"Cabell."

The line was silent and there was only the noise of the static over it and the storm outside.

"She is with me," Jack said.

"Who is with you?" Woolworth said. "What in the hell are you talking about?"

Colette had come into the store. Jack beckoned to her and she walked over. He handed her the phone. She said hello to her father and stood there listening to him. Jack could hear his voice coming garbled through the earpiece. He took the phone back.

"You bring her back here or I will have the state troopers," Woolworth said.

"I have a gun," Jack said.

"You're crazy."

Jack didn't say anything, listened.

"Oh, my God, he's crazy," Woolworth murmured, although whether to himself or to someone standing nearby Jack couldn't tell.

"Leave that university stuff alone until tonight," Jack said.

"Let me speak to her."

"No." Jack's heart was beating very fast and there was only the static coming over the wire.

"What time?" Woolworth said.

"Ten."

"I will meet you at the other place," Woolworth said.

"All right."

"You just take it easy."

"All right."

"Nothing is going to happen," Woolworth said.

"It had better not."

"You just take it easy. You bring her on in and we'll talk."

Jack didn't reply.

"Let me talk to her again," Woolworth said.

"No," Jack said, and hung up.

The proprietor accosted them as they were leaving the store.

"You want some straw hats?" he asked.

"No," Jack said.

"You had better get you some straw hats. All the young folks is wearing them."

"No, thanks," Jack said.

"It will keep the storm off you."

"No, thank you," Jack said. As he went out to the car he heard the man on the radio shouting, but he could not make out what was being said.

"What was that all about?" Colette asked.

"Nothing."

She was looking at him in a way he didn't like.

"Tell me about your horse," he said. But she didn't answer.

The rain was pounding down in sheets and the wipers did not clear off the windows. Jack drove along slowly, hunched up to the windshield and peering out. At last he pulled the car over to the side and stopped the motor.

"What is the matter with you?" she said.

He sat there for a long time, looking at the blurred light patterns the streaking rain made.

"I can't take it any more," he said.

"Can't take what?"

"I want you to marry me."

"Please, Jack, I don't want to argue about that any more," she said.

He sat there staring at the rain.

"I am already married, Jack," she said.

"That doesn't count."

"My God, Jack, what has it got to do to count?"

"I don't know," he said.

"It has counted, Jack, more than I am ever going to tell you." The rain was very heavy. It was thick and close in the car, and the windows were fogged by their breath.

"We will drive down to Alabama," he said. "You can get the divorce Monday."

Colette reached for his hand. He moved it away.

"Jack," she said, "it has got to end sometime."

"No."

"We can't go to Alabama, Jack."

He didn't say anything.

"Listen," she said. "You don't want me. I sleep with Bill all the time."

He knew her so well. He had known her so well and so long. He hated her and loved her both and was frightened. He was sorry money was mixed up in all this. He believed that if it hadn't been for the money, the trouble never would have happened in the first place. He wished there were one good thing in his life money wasn't mixed up in.

"You still think it never happened, don't you?" she said.

"Listen," he said, "there is nothing wrong with a man thinking any way it helps him to think."

She unhooded her eyes for him now and spoke in a rational tone. "Live like that," she said, "and you'll go crazy."

"Everybody thinks like I do. Everybody lives like I do. You have got to believe the things that it is good for you to believe."

"But that's intellectually dishonest."

"No ma'am. What is so is what you think is so. Besides, I have got to have food to eat and a place to live in and work to do. Then I can worry about the intellectually honest part of it if I want to pick up a hobby. I am just like everybody else."

"You can't establish a marriage on intellectual dishonesty," she said. "You can't base anything on that."

"That's right," he said. "You base things on money."

"My money, if we go to Alabama."

"It doesn't matter whose," he said. "Later on it will be my money. I will make a lot of money."

"Yes, and hate me all my life."

"I am asking you to marry me."

She was frightened in an intolerable way.

"Well, let's just have it out right now," she said.

"All right."

"Because I am not going to Alabama and I am not going to marry you and if you had ten million dollars I wouldn't. I have got my life and I chose it and I'll take the consequences of my life. And you had better learn to do the same."

"It would be a lot easier to learn that if I had some money."

"You're crazy. You're already crazy."

He shook his head. "No, I'm not," he said. "You are the one who is crazy."

"Either way," she said. "It doesn't make any difference."

They sat there for a long time in silence, looking at the fogged windshield. Jack was wishing to himself that he had some money so that he could afford to be moral. It would be an exciting hobby, being moral, and he could have philosophical conversations like this with others who were equally moral. He had read somewhere that everybody ought to have a hobby.

After a while the rain stopped and the air was sweet and fresh.

Colette reached over and patted his hand where the signet ring was worn up close to the cut.

"You don't belong in Virginia," she said. "You will be better off in Cincinnati or Denver or someplace."

He got the car moving again. He did not know what he was going to do. In between the car and the mountains a swarm of buzzards was spiraling down. Jack could not see what they were after, but he knew their ways. Soon they would land and gorge themselves and when dusk fell they would rise from the meal and fly back to the mountaintops on which they had lived for tens of thousands of years.

He drove on for a long time. After an hour the dirt road came to a T with a macadam road and he turned right. There were a lot of cars on the macadam road, mostly moving in the direction Jack was. Then there were more cars and soon he was bumper to bumper in the traffic. The traffic passed slowly through a little town whose name he didn't know, crossed over the Rapidan River, and now they went even more slowly, two or three miles an hour. There were many cars parked along the shoulders of the road. People with cameras were walking toward someplace up ahead. Jackbooted state troopers directed traffic, trying to keep the people on foot from walking in front of the cars. Then the traffic halted altogether and Jack sat there looking out the window. Colette was asleep. There was a rocky stream running parallel to the road, about twenty-five yards away, and a man in hip boots was out in the middle of the stream, fishing. The people on foot were lined along the road next to the barbed-wire fence, taking his picture or just looking at him. It was the President of the United States. He had a bright red face, and what seemed to be permanently squinted eyes, and was intent on the fishing. He did not pay any attention to the spectators up on the road. There were some other men in business suits standing behind him on the bank. Some of them were watching him fish while others watched the spectators up on the road. Then the troopers got the cars moving and Jack drove on.

There was no place to go, unless of course you were a buzzard, or rich. The land was so vast and yet there was no place to go. Jack had been to the university and had been taught the courses that explained why it was reasonable and just that there should be millions of persons with no place to go, but he had never truly understood why it was reasonable and just, nor gotten used to the way things were. They were passing a field now that would hold a hundred thousand men, Jack supposed, and there were many fields like it reaching back to the mountains, but you could not go out there and pitch a tent or put up a cabin. Of course, he had heard the reasons for this, too, although it had occurred to him more than once that when Cornelius Cabell had come over in 1654 it was looked upon as good citizenship if you did something like that. Now they would call it insanity. What was deemed sane kept changing, like the weather. Only the weather, after turning bad, would turn good again. But this other thing seemed to be proceeding in one direction only. The road was dry and it had not rained here, but black clouds were coming in over the mountains.

Jack drove into Rappahannock. First there was the

nigger town in the hollow, nothing more than a few shanties gathered around the nigger church. Up on the hill the white town began, with the old stone houses abutting directly on the road. Beyond that was the newer white section, houses built since the War Between the States. In the middle of town, between the old and new sections, was a Gulf filling station and a grocery store with a Hershey Ice Cream sign outside on which it said ACK-WARDS. Across the street from that was a gigantic oak tree with a little marker out front which had been put there by the Daughters of the Confederacy. The marker had "Cabell" chiseled at the top of it and some lettering underneath that was too small to make out.

Jack pulled in next to the pump and went inside the grocery store, passing on his way the half-dozen overalled men sitting out on the bench. There was a cooler inside and Jack reached down into the ice water and got his hand on the Coca-Colas. The water was very cold and when he took the colas out they frosted up in his hands. He paid for them with a couple of nickels and went out on the front porch. He stood there drinking a Coca-Cola and looking at the huge oak across the road. All its limbs were healthy and the dark-green leaves were just beginning to turn yellow. Beyond it were the blue mountains. More clouds had come over the mountains and were moving toward the village. It was warm now, warm and humid up here. Colette was huddled against the passenger door, her eyes closed. The Coca-Cola was ice cold and stung Jack's whiskey-dried mouth. He tried to remember how long it had been since he'd slept.

From up toward the new end of town now there came explosions like firecrackers popping.

"He's still carrying on," a man on the porch said.

Jack walked over to the car, woke Colette, handed her a Coke.

"Where are we?" she asked.

"Rappahannock."

"I remember now. Good God."

The gas pump stopped its grinding and everything was still. The attendant's feet crunched loudly on the gravel.

"You had best be careful driving up through that part of town," he said. "There's a fellow shooting."

"Hunting?" Jack asked.

"No, sir," the attendant said. "Shooting a gun out of the window. They've got the doctor up there with him, but he won't let him in."

"Why not call the police?" Colette asked.

"Don't have any," the attendant said.

"My God," she murmured. "How can you have civilization without police?"

Jack put the car in gear and drove slowly up toward the newer part of town. Now the popping noises were louder. Up on the right, across from the schoolhouse, was a large white stucco house with dark-green shutters. Three men and a woman stood behind a pump house in the yard. Jack looked up at the house and saw smoke drifting away from an open dormer window. He turned up a steep drive that led to a schoolhouse.

Up on the schoolhouse hill, Jack turned the car around and looked down. Now there was more shooting and more white smoke coming from the dormer window.

I understand that man, Jack thought. Whatever his reasons, I understand him better than I do my own father.

Emerging now from under the limbs of the Cabell tree was the yellow and black snout of a Charlottesville taxicab. It stopped along the shoulder of the road a hundred yards short of the house. The passenger door opened and Phoebe got out and began walking toward the house.

So that is it, Jack thought. That is why she will go anywhere.

By now the man with the pistol had climbed out on the roof and was firing into the air. He was a broadshouldered, powerfully built blackhaired man and he was stripped to the waist. Now the girl walked past the people in the yard and stood looking up at him. The man was yelling something at her and waving his hand for her to go away. Then, abruptly, he put his hand up to his face, covering his eyes. The girl continued to look up at him. Presently the man climbed back through the window and she went on into the house.

Meanwhile the curly-headed fellow had gotten out of the taxicab, climbed the fence, and gone to stand with the others behind the pump house, out of the line of fire.

Jack took his coat off and hung it on the car's headlamp and began to stroll down the hill toward where the fellow was. He was murderously angry.

8

"You don't ever come to see me no more," Phoebe's father said. He was sitting cross-legged on top of the chest of drawers in the bedroom he had all to himself and the pistol was lying over in the corner where he'd flung it. He had an open, full bottle of whiskey clutched in his hand. Phoebe went over to him now and he reached down awkwardly and hugged her. He was an awkward man, almost clumsy when he was around his daughter, and she was intensely fond of him. The room smelled of gunpowder.

"I have had too much to drink, is all," he said.

"No, you haven't."

"I have, too. I have had plenty to drink. This ain't the only bottle. There are plenty of other bottles."

"No, there aren't."

"There are, too," he said.

She sat there looking up at him. He seemed beautiful to her.

"Have you been building any houses?" she asked.

He shook his head. "No," he said.

"Well, you will be building some soon."

"I have been doing some remodeling."

"Where?"

"Over at Little Washington," her father said. There were mud spatters on his cuffs, mud on his shoes.

"I have been working right hard," he said. He looked off a little to the side as he talked to her. Something had happened to his sight a few years back; he was almost blind and could see things better if he did not look at them directly. He had lambent, gentle blue eyes and they were not looking right at her but she knew he was seeing her as best he could.

"What have you been doing?" he asked.

"Going to school," she said.

He didn't respond right away and seemed to be watching her. She didn't know how well he could see, just that he couldn't read a book or draw up plans any more, and that glasses did not help.

"I have a nice room," she said.

He nodded.

"Charlottesville is a beautiful place," she said. "I've been to the university and walked over the grounds and Bill and Colette took me up to Monticello."

Her father climbed down off the chest of drawers, put on a shirt and began buttoning it. "Has anybody been bothering you?" he asked.

"No," she said. "Everyone is as nice as they can be." She listened to herself saying that; or rather the voice saying it through her.

"I have been having some bad dreams," he said. "I dreamed some feller was bad to you."

"Everything is fine, really," she said.

"You let me know if anybody is ever bad to you," he said.

"Don't worry," she said. "I will."

He retrieved the revolver and stuck it in his belt.

"Did you get something to eat?" he asked.

"No, I'm fine, really," she said.

He opened the door for her and they left the bedroom and went downstairs. He was walking behind her. As they reached the landing she looked through the window and saw that the state trooper's automobile had pulled up in the front yard.

When they got down to the first floor her father put his arm around her and hugged her. She was crying.

"I'm sorry," she said. She had planned not to cry this time but she could not help it. "I'm sorry for whatever it is," she said.

"That is all right," he said. He was patting her on the back in that clumsy way he had. "There is nothing wrong with me," he said.

"If I knew what it was I would do something," she said.

"There is nothing wrong with me," her father said. "Don't you worry about me."

I am not going to any more, she thought. I can't.

"Play me some of them songs that woman taught you," he said.

"Which woman?"

"You know, that piano teacher of yours."

"Mrs. Ross?"

"Yes."

"All right," she said. "But I had better go outside first."

She walked out on the lawn and around the other side of the pump house. Her mother was sitting in a lawn chair talking to Pat Roosevelt and a man whose head she couldn't see because of the high back of the lawn chair he was sitting in. His fingers drummed on the chair arm. A little off to the side, the young state trooper was talking urgently to the doctor, Codd.

"We just can't have this kind of thing in Rappahannock County any more," the trooper said.

Codd's little brown eyes were glittering out at the trooper from under his bushy gray brows. "I don't know why not," he said. "We have had it for three hundred years, ever since there have been Virginians."

"You don't seem to understand," the trooper said. "Hell, the President of the . . ." Then he saw Phoebe.

"I beg your pardon, ma'm," he said.

"That's all right," Phoebe said.

"I didn't see you, ma'm," the trooper said.

"That's all right."

"Is your father going to the hospital voluntarily?"

"No."

"That is his right," Codd said. "It is his own fool property."

"You don't understand," the trooper said. "We have got the President of the United States in this county."

"I don't see what that has to do with it," Codd said. Behind him Phoebe saw her mother still talking to the two men, as if nothing had happened.

"People are looking to this country," the trooper said. "Foreign nations are looking to this country."

"How old are you?" Codd asked.

"Twenty-one."

"Well, that explains it."

"I have got to take him in," the trooper said.

Codd shook his head. "No."

The trooper stood there looking back and forth from Codd to Phoebe.

"Go on and drive your car," Codd said. "You have still got plenty of driving around to do in your car before it gets dark."

The sky was black over the mountains now and Phoebe saw a lightning flash split the blackness. There was a storm over in the Shenandoah Valley and it was coming over the mountains.

She went into the house again. Her father was sitting in a straight-back chair near the piano. She sat down at the keyboard and lifted the lid. It smelled musty as pianos do when they've not been used, and the keys were hard to strike. She asked him what he wanted to hear, but he said he couldn't remember the names of any of the songs. She began to play "Alice Blue Gown." Her fingers felt stiff and unnatural and slipped in the cracks between the keys. Then she played it a second time. Now it was better, and she knew that if she kept on playing it would improve until it was effortless—or rather, devoid of distracted effort. Then she could get lost down in the music and control it at the same time. She had discovered this about playing the piano years ago, that it worked that way. All you had to do was want to play, and be willing to play awkwardly, and keep at it. Then the playing would improve and you could keep on until you got tired.

Cheated on an examination.

You had to have faith and perseverence, she thought, although she did not use those words in thinking about it. But she knew how playing a piano worked and supposed that other things worked in the same way. She had thought that Pat Roosevelt worked in the same way and had gone to live with him in New York believing that if she kept at it, it would smooth out. And she had kept at it, all right, but it had not smoothed out. But the piano playing still worked that way.

Cheated on an examination.

"I am thinking of going back to New York," she said now over her playing.

107

"Stop," her father said.

She let her hands rest on the keys.

"I thought you said you were thinking about going back to New York."

"That's right," Phoebe said. "Tonight."

"No. You are not going back to any New York," her father said.

"I have to," she said. "For a little while. Otherwise I am just going to be a secretary the rest of my life."

"I don't understand what that has got to do with it," he said.

"I don't want to be a secretary," she said. "And I don't want to live with Bill any more. It's like living out on the sidewalk. It's not safe there. It's not safe anywhere."

Her father was quiet for a long time.

"There is no help for that," he said at last.

She wanted him to forbid her, absolutely, to go back to New York.

"You don't have to worry about the money," she said. "I've arranged to borrow the money."

Pat had stopped the cab along the way and told her about the faculty appointment at the University of South Carolina. He had shown her some new photographs of the mansion, too. It was a most distinguished-looking mansion, Phoebe thought. She had forgotten how nice it was. She and Pat had taken a walk through the fields while Bill waited at the car. She found she'd forgotten about Pat, too: how winning and attractive he was.

"You are not going to New York," her father said. "You can do anything else but you are not going to New York."

This was not strong enough for her. What she wanted him to say was that if she went to New York he would come and bring her back, and she tried to make herself push him into saying that. But she couldn't do it. He is stricken, she thought. He was feeling bad before I came here and I am just making it worse.

"You can come back here," he said.

"No, I can't, Daddy."

"There are lots of young fellows around here."

She knew that. On her way into town she'd seen them sitting on Ackwards' front porch spitting tobacco juice over the railing.

She sat there on the piano bench, looking at her father. This is it, she thought. I am going to decide. I thought I would have two more years before I had to, but I am going to decide now, this afternoon. And the rest of my life will just be the playing out of what I decide now. There will be no more decisions that amount to anything. I am still all right and I will be broken in and it will be all right because I am like the piano, not the player, and when I am broken in it will be all right.

As the state trooper's car was pulling out of the driveway,
Jack stood up. And was going to have Roosevelt stand up,
too. But Pat and Bill had gone on into the house, and the
men who'd been standing in the shelter of the pump
house drifted away. Only the fellow in the white linen suit
was left, and he stood there on the lawn, lighting a black
cigar, cupping the match against the storm wind that was
whipping down smartly from the mountains.

Presently the big blackhaired man, the one who'd been
doing the shooting, came out of the house and across the
lawn and stood talking with the man in the linen suit.
Colette had already ambled down the schoolhouse hill
and gone inside.

Jack was there alone, sitting in a lawn chair, looking up
the schoolhouse hill to where his car was parked with the
jacket hung over a headlight. Behind it the black storm
was moving down the mountain. After a while the man
in the white suit left and went strolling back toward town
with the wind whipping at his trousers cuffs.

The big fellow saw Jack, came over, and sat down. He

was carrying a bottle of whiskey in his trousers pocket and he took it out now and passed it to Jack, who took a big drink and handed it back to the man, who did likewise.

"I don't give a damn, do you, young feller?" the big man said.

"No," Jack said.

Now the first patter of rain began and Jack sat there in the lawn chair feeling the whiskey burn his throat and belly; then the warmth came back up. The big man passed the whiskey bottle to him and he took another drink. A lightning bolt arrowed sizzling down on the schoolhouse hill with an almost simultaneous explosion of thunder and now the rain swept on them in waves and Bill London was running toward them across the lawn holding a coat over his head and yelling to his father, "For God's sake, come on in." But Old Man Jim just proffered the whiskey bottle to him and there was another flash/bang! off to the side and Bill London shook his head and went running tiptoe back to the house with the coat over his head and Jack sat there already drenched and hardly able to see the big man because of the water pouring over his forehead and down into his eyes, conscious only of the wet bottle being passed to him together with the big man's laughter which came loud and hearty now and Jack took another drink and handed the bottle back and now there were three or four people yelling out to them from the porch. Jack and the big man sat there in the rain torrents for five or ten minutes, whipped by the wind, and the lightning struck several times near them and the rain beat down heavily. After a while there was no one on the front porch calling out to them any more and they were alone together on the lawn chairs near the pump house. Then the lightning began striking farther away and in a few minutes it was gone. Now there was only an occasional far rumble as the storm moved toward the coast. Then the rain, too, was gone and they were sitting there.

"I don't know what it's all about, young feller," Jim London said.

But Jack was thinking, Maybe you don't and maybe you do.

They were there in the wet yard together, listening to the storm retreat. There was a cool breeze now and no sounds from the house. It was getting dark and the lights in the house had come on. The windows shone. Soon an automobile with its lights on came down the road and turned into the driveway. A small, manicured hand waved out of the window to them and the car drove on up to the house.

"That is my son," Jim said. "He has been to Philadelphia."

Jack had been watching the big man, and wondering, as he did with all men, whether he could take him. This man was very powerful and moved with great confidence and there was that thing in his eyes which said that if you did take him you would have to kill him to do it. He was an unusual man, Jack thought.

"He has been on a shopping trip," the big man said. "His mother wanted him to go on a shopping trip."

They were together for a long time. Dusk made the clouds even darker. Then it was night. The house's windows shone brightly.

"Every man thinks he knows what is right," Old Man Jim said out of the darkness.

"Yes, sir."

"Or if he doesn't know, he thinks there is someplace he can go and find out."

"Yes, sir."

"He will die thinking that."

He will more likely die sooner if he thinks that, Jack said to himself.

"An old fellow told me one time that the only way to be happy was never to want something somebody didn't want to give you," Jim said. "And I thought that was pretty smart. But I have never been able to live up to it."

Jack didn't say anything.

"But I will tell you what I read in a book," Jim said. "About the world. It is 'self-interest, ferocity, and fine words.' Did I say it right?"

"What?"

" 'Ferocity.' "

"I think so," Jack said.

"I read that out of a book," Jim London said.

Six of them were inside sitting around the dining room table: Pat Roosevelt, Bill, Colette, Phoebe, her mother, and her kid brother, Peter, who had just come back from Philadelphia with the new table game. They had read the rules and they were now playing the new game. There was a lot of colored paper money and there were little counters you moved around the edge of the board and tiny green houses made out of painted wood and red hotels, slightly larger. Every time Phoebe made her move she would run upstairs and do some packing and then she would come running back down the stairs, roll the dice, make her move, and then run back up the stairs.

Pat Roosevelt had six hotels now and plenty of money. He was playing generously. He would collect in full when someone landed on a property occupied by a hotel, but he did not collect the smaller fees on undeveloped property. Not having to deal in smaller bills made for a smoother game, he thought.

Phoebe had not said flatly that she was going with him,

but he knew from the packing that she would. They would go to New York and meet his parents and fly down to South Carolina for the wedding. Given the condition of her father, it would have to be that way, Pat supposed, although he would just as soon have had the wedding in Rappahannock, maybe under the historic old tree. He was looking forward to visiting here with his bride, and already felt himself to be part of this Southern family. It made him feel good. He was marrying the South. It was not any accident of birth but something he had chosen to be.

Cabell was standing beside him.

"I would like to see you for just a minute," Jack said.

Pat smiled at the others, excused himself, and followed Cabell into the living room.

"Outside," Jack said.

Pat reached out his hand to put on Cabell's shoulder and it was smacked violently away. Pat stood there, poised and looking at him. "Let me give you some good advice," he said. "You don't want to see me outside, or any place else." With that, he went back to the dining room and resumed his place at the game board.

Thinking, I know the type. If anybody in the world knows that type, I do. That is what she would have ended up marrying if I hadn't come back to save her. That is the rival, too.

Now Jack, who was drenched, stood in the archway between the living room and the dining room. When Phoebe went upstairs, Jack waited a minute, looking at Roosevelt. Then went up after her.

She was packing a suitcase and it was mostly full. She was wearing something around her neck he hadn't seen before, an arrowhead on a leather thong. She smiled when she saw him, a troubled smile. She saw him looking at the arrowhead.

114

"My father gave this to me when I was a little girl," she said.

She was really very beautiful. The room was small.

"I enjoyed meeting you," she said.

Jack didn't say anything, just stood there.

"I have something I want to give you," she said. On the top of her dresser was a gold pocket watch and she handed it to him. It was surprisingly heavy.

"I want you to have this," she said. "It belonged to your great-uncle."

Pat Roosevelt was standing in the doorway. "It's your turn," he said. He stood there.

"Where are you going?" Jack asked the girl.

"I have to play," she said.

Jack didn't touch her, didn't dare touch her, stepped back. She stood in the doorway and was looking at him.

"I am going away," she said.

Jack couldn't think of anything to say. She turned and went downstairs and he stood there hefting the watch in his hand.

Bill and Colette came up the stairs and went into the room across the hall.

Pat was eating some fried chicken. Belle London had prepared a little plate of it and put it by his elbow. The crust was brown and delicious and there were hot buttered biscuits with it. Only three of them were left at the table: Phoebe, who was making her move, Pat, and the kid brother, Peter London. Phoebe landed on "Go," collected two hundred dollars, and went upstairs. Now Pat was alone with the kid brother.

"I wanted to go to Mars today," Peter said. He was a delicate, sensitive-looking boy, well dressed and well groomed.

"Is that a town?" Pat asked.

"The planet, Mars," Peter London said. "I kept thinking, I have got to get to Mars. But then I'd think, I can't get to Mars."

"I know what you mean," Pat said.

"But then I'd think, I *have* to get to Mars," the kid brother said. He did something with his eyes that said will you and Roosevelt's eyes said no.

"This sure is some mighty good fried chicken, Miz London," Pat said.

"At least close the door," Bill London said.

"No," Colette said. She was doing the thing he liked. He liked the same thing that Jack did.

"Good God, he is right across the hall," Bill said.

"I know," she mumbled. She was looking Cabell in the eye and had been doing so ever since she'd reached out her free hand to swing open the door.

Phoebe came back into the room and Jack was standing there with the watch in his hand looking at the door across the hall, which had just been closed.

"You see, it has your coat of arms on it," she said. On the watch's face were the five silver diamonds on the red shield, the fleurs-de-lis, the elephant's head surmounting in green and gold. With the Latin for "Faithful and Grateful" on the shield.

"I want you to marry me," Jack said.

Phoebe turned and walked out of the room. Jack followed her. When she got to the foot of the stairs she did not return to her place at the dining room table but turned and went into the kitchen and through the door down into the cellar, with Jack following her. There was a kerosene lantern burning in the cellar and there were shelves of preserved fruits and vegetables from floor to ceiling three walls around and the kerosene light shone on the glass jars. Thick-peppered hams hung from the ceiling and Jack could smell them. Up against the bare wall was an old sofa and Phoebe sat down on it and leaned back on the base of her spine and rested her neck on top of the sofa and lay slumped there gazing dully at the shelves of preserved fruits and vegetables and not saying anything. Jack was standing on the steps looking at her. A long time passed.

"You could say something," he said. "You could tell me whether you will consider it."

"I am considering it."

Another great while passed.

Presently the kitchen door opened and her father came down the cellar stairs, went into his plans room, and shut the door. Still Phoebe half lay there looking up at the shelves and not saying anything.

"I have got to know tonight," Jack said.

"Someone told me you cheated on your examinations," she said.

"That's a damned lie," Jack said.

She looked at him. "Is it?"

"Yes."

"I just can't understand why anybody would lie about a thing like that."

"Listen," he said, "we are living in a world where anybody will lie about anything."

"I know," she said. She half lay there looking at him. She was watching his mouth.

"I give you my word of honor I didn't," he said.

She looked at him for a long time. "I suppose the answer's yes," she said.

He didn't kiss her. It was too serious and important for that.

"Let's go," he said.

"Where?"

"First Charlottesville, then Maryland."

"You mean tonight?"

"Yes."

"We can't do that. I hardly even know you. We have to get to know each other first." She got up and climbed past him on the steps and went through the kitchen and up to her room again. Everything was packed. She closed the suitcase. Her mother came in.

"What are you going to do?" her mother asked.

"I don't know."

"Why not stay here for a little while? And think things over."

I have been thinking things over for nineteen years and it has done me no good, Phoebe thought. All I know is I can't be here and I can't be in Charlottesville with Bill and I have got to decide.

Bill came into the room and stood there behind his mother, tucking in his shirttails.

"What is going on?" he asked.

"I don't know," his mother said.

"Tell Cabell to go back where he came from," he told Phoebe.

Phoebe didn't answer him. She didn't know what she was going to do. Thinking, I am going to decide and it will never be the same again no matter what it is. Only I do not want to get married tonight.

"Why not tell him yourself?" she said.

"I have got to talk to Daddy, is why," Bill said. "Daddy is very sick and I want you to get that cheater out of here."

10

Old Man Jim sat at the desk in his plans room. He could not read any of the blueprints piled there, had been unable to do that for the half dozen years now since he'd bought and drunk some bad moonshine whiskey. His wife read the blueprints for him now and handled the correspondence and the payroll and anything else that required reading. So it was not a plans room any more in the original sense it had been called that, although he still did his planning there, alone in the evenings, and during the day his wife, who had become a skilled draftsman, would draw the plans from his dictation; which was minutely complete in all dimensions and with elevations and angles given. He was possibly the best architect in Virginia, better than Bill London would ever be. Although he was relatively unknown in his own lifetime because he had not gone to the University of Virginia or any university but had taught himself architecture while he was a master carpenter. Which was the way he'd started out in Rappahannock a quarter century before.

He spent most of the time he was at home alone out

in the front yard or sitting alone down here. His wife did not speak to him except about the plans and the payroll and other business matters. He did not have any visitors except for Codd, the town's doctor, who would drop in every couple of weeks and sit down there in the plans room smoking the black cigars and talking about whatever enthusiasm was possessing him at the moment. For a while Codd had been raising goldfish and then for a year he had cultivated African violets and for the past summer had been playing chess by mail. Jim knew nothing of the chess and was unable to envision it or appreciate who Mr. Capablanca was, although he had enjoyed the African violets and the goldfish. He was even glad to hear about the chess, because the talk of a good man, he had found, was like music, and you could enjoy it without having to listen to the words.

He did not know what he was going to do about his daughter, but he had not talked to Codd about that, nor to anyone else. Codd would come and leave and Jim would be left with the aroma of expensive cigar smoke, and the questions he could not answer and the plans he had made but could not read. He was not a smoker himself, but he loved the smell of a fine cigar.

There was a knock on the door now and his son came in, Bill.

"Daddy, you have got to go to the hospital," Bill said.

"No," Jim said. The boy was sitting on the corner of the desk and Jim could see the blur of him out of the corner of his eye.

"You have got to, Daddy. They have doctors now that can make you better."

"It's no use talking about it," Jim said.

"But you're embarrassing Mother terribly. You just don't realize."

"Listen, son," Jim said. "There is nothing wrong with shooting a gun if you feel like doing it."

"But I am the head of the family now," Bill said. "And I have got to think about the rest of us."

"Do you want a drink?"

"No, sir."

I had better not have one, either, Jim thought. Not with him. I had better not have one now or he will tell the troopers that I have drunk myself crazy.

"I am only thinking about the family," Bill said.

"How about you, young feller?" Jim asked. "How are you getting along?"

"Swell," Bill said.

"Your family is all right?"

"It's swell, Dad, swell."

"I will bet you are mighty proud of that good-looking wife of yours," Jim said.

"Yes, sir."

"You-all ought to come up and see me."

"We have been pretty busy," Bill said.

"It is only fifty miles."

"Well, we are pretty busy. I am on the Honor Council now."

"What is that?" Jim asked.

"We enforce the honor code," Bill said. "You know, we protect the integrity of the school."

Jim had a paperweight on his desk, a crystalline Virginia diamond. He hefted that in his hand and felt its smooth planed surfaces on his palm and fingertips. He had found it on an unusual morning in the yard of a certain cottage out on the Marshall road, and he believed it had power in it, intelligence. Sometimes he would hold it in his hand when he was planning his houses.

"You are a good boy," he said. "I am proud of you."

121

Thinking to himself, Yes, proud of you like I was proud of the cotton mill floor I swept clean when I was twelve years old and working in the mills and which since has been swept fifty thousand times. But still proud. Jim was always embarrassed when this son talked about the "family," especially since Bill had stopped speaking to him when he was thirteen or fourteen years old; that is, had stopped speaking to him except for giving advice.

Jim got up now, went over to the window, fumbled with the latch, opened it. The sweet cool smell that comes after a rain was lilting in now over the sill.

"Live your own life," he said. "You can live it here if you want. I will build you a house anywhere in town you want and you can work with me and you can have supper over here and we can go fishing and you can live here in this house if you want and you don't even have to come out of your bedroom. You can hide in there. But you live your own life. I don't know what good it does you if you don't live it. I am forty-eight years old and you are not going to live mine."

There was a tap on the door now and it was Pat Roosevelt. He had gone out to the taxi and put on a fresh white shirt and a tie with regimental stripes and a freshly pressed coat and he stood there clean and handsome with his shoes shined.

"I would like to speak with Mr. London," he said, and Bill left.

Pat had practiced this scene all the way down on the train. He had thought about it many times before getting on the train, too. He would get dressed in his most honest and straightforward clothes and he would speak manfully and honestly in his South Carolina accent. Now as he was beginning he heard someone running down the stairs and it was Bill again, who burst in and said, "They've gone."

Which turned out to be true; there was no suitcase on Phoebe's bed, no car parked up on schoolhouse hill.

This, too, was something Pat had provided for, daydreamed about. Indeed, he liked it even better than the part about asking the father for her hand in marriage. Because the best daydream of all, and one he'd had repeatedly, was of fighting for her. The only trouble with that dream had been that somebody else would have to provoke the fight because Roosevelt played by the rules (which were made for men like himself) and outside of high school and college wrestling matches had never fought anybody in his life.

But now he jumped in the taxicab and set out after Cabell. He was sure the fellow was headed back toward Charlottesville, to a party, probably, one of those wild University of Virginia drinking parties. And so now Pat set out after him on the black nightslick road, picking up speed as he passed the little light that shone out of Ackwards' and on the underside of the leaves of the tree across the street from it, picking up speed out into the black countryside and with Bill and Colette riding in the seat behind him. It was thrilling, just what he'd come down South for, and Pat Roosevelt was, to himself, at the minimum, John Singleton Mosby, speeding through the night in the service of a cause that would justify any kind of honorable violence. It is for her own good, he told himself. That fellow Cabell is a criminal. It is written on his face.

I will remember this all the rest of my life, Pat thought. When Phoebe and I are sitting on the front porch of the plantation celebrating our golden wedding anniversary and with our children and grandchildren all around us I will remember this. That will be 1981. I will get her back and I will be gentle this time although not with him.

Jack and Phoebe were alone together now for the first time. The few minutes at the breakfast table that morning had not counted (not to Jack) and the drive down to Louisa had not counted because he had been drunk then and, at the time, she had played no part in his plans beyond the stray thought of screwing her for revenge. Besides, to Jack's way of looking at it, there was something about daytime that fixed it so that you could not be alone with anybody then; light hurtled in from all directions and with it the world.

But it was night now, cloud-hung black night. Jack and Phoebe were together in the cockpit of the car with only the low glow of the instrument panel and the headlights arrowing out in front of them; alone together now in the little moving tin room that was their first home, the only one they could afford. And they were together only tenuously, because nothing had been truly resolved. Although they'd left her family's place together, walking out on the sun deck over the pump house and climbing down to the ground after the thrown suitcase. Nothing had been settled because Phoebe wanted an engagement and a church wedding and above all she wanted sanity. Which to her way of thinking was possible only when things moved much more slowly than they were moving now.

Because it had not been more than twenty-six hours since she'd first clapped eyes on him, unless you counted the momentary glimpse she'd gotten as he moved toward the bindle stiff with the crowd already closing in and blocking him from view. And she would not be with him now if she'd been able to see the fight. She had no idea of what he was.

She suspected him of nothing. Her reluctance to marry him this very evening had nothing to do with that. It was just that it did not seem sane to do it this evening and she wanted above all to be sane. She did not mind the whore-house part and she tended to believe him about not having cheated on the examinations. The more she thought about it, the more she watched his handsome profile in the dashboard's glow, the more she believed him, and by the time they passed through Little Washington and Sperryville, she believed him completely. She could tell from his face that he would never do a thing like that. He was honorable, handsome, and of the perfect family, and by marrying him she would be claiming as legal and true the secret name she'd always called herself, from as early as she could remember: *Phoebe Cabell.* She had thought, as a little girl, that possibly there had been some midwife's mistake, mysterious circumstances, true parents elsewhere.

And so the dark and dimly lit lone tin room in which she sat by Jack's side now mostly in silence moved through the night with Pat Roosevelt pursuing, although neither of them had considered the possibility of that, so absorbed were Phoebe and Jack in carrying out whatever negotiations were unresolved between them, which centered around the question of whether they were to be married that night. And therefore included the question as to whether they would be married at all.

"Not tonight," she said.

Jack didn't respond, just went on driving, but he had her now so that he could answer her wordlessly and looking at his face in the dashboard's glow she saw the "Yes, tonight," as clearly as if he'd said it out loud.

"Not tonight," she repeated, and his face gave her the same answer. They were having a quarrel, and one to which Jack was not devoting his full attention. Because he was sure that by now Woolworth had the state police out and at every turnoff on the road he was looking for the darkened trooper car. They all had radios now. At the same time his mind was running ahead to the meeting with Woolworth.

In the town of Madison Jack had a great-uncle, his grandmother's brother, who was a lawyer. But Jack drove on through that town without stopping for advice or even slowing down. He had spent too much time getting advice, he believed. Now he had all the advice he needed and he would have to make up his own mind; the days of boyhood having died that morning on the front porch of the Louisa hotel, or so he thought.

He would use Negro cunning now, criminal lore, but he would use it in his own way and not ask for any more advice. He would force his way through and he would even kill Jefferson Woolworth if he had to, and he would smash or circumvent anything that got in his way including the girl who rode with him now in the front seat of his grandfather's car. He was committed, not as a motion-picture saint gazing dreamily at the sky is committed, but the way a halfback who has sprinted out and made his cut is. It was a question of momentum. If he believed in anything it was what the crazy man had said to him in the front yard. Yes, he believed it the way you believe your hole card is the ace of spades when you pick up the corner and see that it is the ace of spades. He no longer entertained any other possibilities. He was determined to survive because he loved pussy and whiskey too much to die.

He believed that the girl—what was her name?—would sense this fatal determination in him and that it would override all her objections. Which was vital, because she was central to any plan he had left that did not call for killing Woolworth. He thought she must be pretty hard up to consider marrying him, quick like that, and he reflected to himself that she might not be so much of a prize as she seemed to be. There is more to her than I know, he thought.

He didn't care whether the marriage would work out or not. He was too desperate even to think about that. He would see that it worked out until he passed the bar examination and if she wanted to bail out then, fine. Thus the argument over whether they would get married tonight, not some other night, was over so far as Jack was concerned. They had to get married tonight or someone would die. He began to sing.

> In the Blue Ridge Mountains of Virginia,
>   On the Trail of the Lonesome Pine,
> Where the pale moon shines, my heart inclines,
>   To where you carved your name, and I carved mine. . . .

As he went into the second verse, Phoebe began singing softly along with him, as they drove together now through the vast darkness down that long arrowing pine-surrounded road, with Pat Roosevelt behind them, intent and gaining, and the Blue Ridge Mountains themselves running down darkly parallel to the little two-lane macadam road like a black ocean wave that has not yet broken and is never going to break. Fall was coming off the mountain now, cold air, and they rolled up the windows and were in there alone together in the glow of dashboard light with Pat Roosevelt gaining.

"It's a pretty night," Phoebe said. Jack's coat had been drenched in the storm and she had nothing to put around her shoulders and was very cold.

Old Man Jim put on his mackinaw and went to sit in the front yard. It was cold out there and he jammed his hands down into the pockets. It was dark and the night-wind was pouring off the mountains, making its far low moan through the mountain's trees. There was no other noise, no cars passing. It is so quiet now, Jim thought.

It was always this way after the children left. They came in noisily with their cheerful unhappiness and when they left it was quieter than it had seemed before.

They will never roost anywhere, Jim thought. They do not roost and they live in automobiles and they come here in automobiles to this place that has never moved talking to me about families. They sit at a table playing with little colored pieces of paper and then they tell me about families.

Now there came a droning noise cutting through the treemoaning, getting louder and becoming a snarl as an airplane passed overhead, moving on east toward where Big Washington was. Jim had heard this plane many nights.

Someone was standing there beside him.

"Daddy?" It was the younger son, Peter. "Mother says you should come back in the house."

"After a while," Jim said.

"She says you have to work on the plans."

But Jim liked it out here. He liked the silence and it felt good to have his face cold again and the air cold in his nostrils.

"Why don't you sit down and keep me company?" he said.

"I can't. I'm in the middle of a book."

"Do you remember back when you used to fetch my toolbox for me?" Jim asked.

"Daddy, I'm freezing to death."

"You were just a little bitty fellow, four or five years old, and it was too heavy for you."

"Daddy, it is freezing cold," the boy said. Jim could not see him.

"What are you reading about?" Jim asked.

"Saint-Exupéry, Daddy."

"What is that about?"

"I have got to go in, Daddy."

"All right," Jim said.

He remembered when the boy was four. He himself had been doing a lot of reading in those days. He had been teaching himself to be an architect out of the books the fellow Wright sent him down from Chicago; many of which had nothing openly to do with architecture but which Jim had learned something out of anyway, absorbing these books so deeply into himself that he did not think about them any more nor need to (although there was that one quotation he knew word for word, as a sort of guide and reminder). He did not recall any Saint-Exupéry although he remembered a great deal about a Saint Peter in whose name certain structures had been built and certain principles enunciated that had to do with foundations. Jim had understood what he had read about Saint Peter and remembered it now without remembering the books. But he wished that he could do some more reading now so as to learn something about Saint-Exupéry and thus have something to talk with the boy about. He had not talked with either of his sons in many years, and he regretted it because he had lived through his young manhood hoping to talk to them when they got older. Now, for no special reason, he remembered the tall phonograph record players they sold in Front Royal and wondered whether, if he bought one, they would have some piano music records to sell him to play on them. He was very fond of piano music.

Bill London was glad that Jack Cabell was finally going to get what was coming to him, and only wished that the decencies of the matter would let him be present at the beating. Although even a beating wouldn't do it for Cabell, so far as he was concerned. The man was far too great a criminal for that. Well, Bill thought to himself, he will be kicked out of school, too, when we catch the nigger who sold him the examination papers. That ought to be about enough.

He hated Jack Cabell and it wasn't only because of Colette's visits to the attic. There was just something about the fellow, and being around him or even passing him on the university grounds made Bill feel bad. It didn't make sense. It was only a feeling. But every time he saw Cabell he felt, That fellow is better than I am.

Of course, it made no sense at all, when Bill thought about it rationally, because Cabell never did anything for anybody except himself, was an outlaw from his family, a criminal who hung around with niggers, a cheat, and an adulterer. But seeing him always made Bill feel low and unworthy. He had given it a lot of thought and believed that it might have something to do with the way Cabell kept his mouth shut; spoke to very few people and said no more than what was necessary. He reminded Bill of Old Man Jim. He'll go crazy, too, one of these days, Bill thought. A man has got to talk. What is life if it isn't smiling and talking?

"What's this about cheating?" Colette asked. She was sitting by Bill in the back seat and Pat was driving.

"We have got the goods on him," Bill said. "We just haven't caught up with the girl yet."

"Who is 'we'?" Colette asked.

"Daddy and I."

That was what he called Woolworth—Daddy.

"I must say I'm not surprised to hear it," Pat said. "He looks like the type."

"I think you-all ought to let him alone," Colette said. Her head was on Bill's shoulder and she was deliciously sleepy and it was warm and comfortable in the cab.

"Nothing doing," Bill said.

"God, it just seems so petty," she said. "Either he has learned the law or he hasn't. If he hasn't he'll fail the bar exam. And if he has, that means he learned it. Why not let him finish up and go away in peace?"

"Because I don't like people lying and cheating and stealing," Bill said. "The world is full of people who lie and cheat and steal. And if there is anything that is good about the University of Virginia, that is the soul of the university, it's that you can believe a man's word there."

"It sounds like pretty poor training for life, if you ask me," Colette said.

"Well, I am not going to let him destroy the university," Bill said.

"If one man can destroy it, perhaps it isn't worth saving," she said.

"It's the principle of the thing."

"If he were in your shoes, he'd let you alone," Colette said.

"It isn't my shoes he's been in."

"How childish," Colette said.

"I don't know, Mrs. London," Pat put in. "It would make all the difference in the world if we had the honor system up at Columbia, a gentlemen's system."

"I don't understand," she said. "If you're a gentleman in the first place, you don't need any system. And if you aren't . . ."

"I disagree," Pat said.

"Honor is a private matter, if you ask me," Colette said.

"No," Pat Roosevelt said. "Begging your pardon. But I think it's a public matter. I think that's what America is all about."

"How's that?" Bill asked. He sat forward in the seat. He took things like this very seriously.

The cab was moving rapidly and Colette was glad she was in the back seat; although she wouldn't have minded being in the front seat if she were driving.

"The Founding Fathers wanted the whole country to run on the honor system," Pat said. "That is what the Constitution is all about."

"Yeah," Bill said. "But wouldn't you have to have a nation of gentlemen to do that?"

"No," Pat said. "You just let the gentlemen run things."

"Jesus," Bill said. "I never thought of it like that." It sounded pretty good to him.

"I got the idea from a friend of my father's," Pat said. "We used to talk about it all the time."

"Live and let live is my motto," Colette said.

Up ahead was a ham-serving roadhouse and Pat pulled in there with the taxi's tires scrunching on the gravel, got out, and went inside.

"Did you break it off?" Bill asked.

"What do you think?" she said.

He tried to kiss her but her head was buried too far into his shoulder.

"When are we going to have that baby?" he asked.

She didn't answer. This angered him because he did not believe she could fall asleep so quickly. When that fellow comes back, he said to himself, she will start talking again. It made him unhappy when she pretended not to hear him. Sometimes she did not seem like such a swell pal, after all.

Inside, on the telephone, Pat had reached his party.

"Do you know who this is?" Pat said.

"Gentleman in 404?" a wheezing voice came.

"Yes. Are they ready?"

"Yes, sir."

"Bring them down to the parking lot, the side door, in half an hour," Pat said. He was very excited.

"Yes, sir."

"Did you test them?"

"Yes, sir."

"Half an hour," Pat said, and returned to the taxicab. It was thrilling, really. It would be something to write about.

"Tell us what you've been doing in New York," Colette asked when he got in.

11

Jack did not drive around to the garage, but parked the car out front on Second Street.

It was the first time Phoebe had seen the Cabell house from the side; high on a hill with steep steps going up to it and three tall oak trees in the yard. A big, rambling house, with many lit-up windows, and she walked up the steps beside Jack, not even holding his hand. There had been none of that, nothing. She was excited and the house was large and safe-looking and it was like coming home. She was cold in her summer dress.

They walked up on the porch and went inside, where Jack ushered her into the living room. His grandfather and grandmother were seated on either side of the fireplace. Logs were burning orangely there. The mantel clock was ticking, slowly, as it always had. The old woman had the Bible in her lap and the old man was reading a news magazine about the Japanese army in Manchuria. They quit reading when Phoebe came in, and began to talk to her.

It was comfortably warm and she felt at home here.

Thinking to herself, This is a place where I can hide; this whole house is a place to hide.

She liked the fire. It smelled like some kind of apple wood, whose syrupy scent came out of the log ends in dark-brown bubbles of hissing sap. And she liked the other aroma this house had, too, a certain rich scent of bath soap. Then Dot came in with her fiancé from the university, and the young people and the old people sat around the fire talking. Nobody is crazy here, Phoebe thought. Nobody will bother me here.

Jack was up in the attic, packing. He removed the papers from his law school briefcase and put some shirts and a pair of khaki trousers in it. Then he brought out the rifle, took it over to his desk, and began to clean it. He remembered now that most of the bullets he had were old and might possibly fail to fire. Turning the kerosene lantern up, he took a handful of the bullets from the desk drawer and dumped them rattling in the cone of light the lantern threw on the desk. He saw now that some of the bullets shone more brightly than the others and he loaded the gun with those and put the rest of the bright bullets in his pocket. Then he took the old ones over to the briefcase, dropped them in alongside the shirts, and put on his dry jacket.

Downstairs, Phoebe was deciding, I will take the chance. The family and the house and the smells had excited her to it. I will take a chance and do it, she thought, because what is honor if it isn't taking chances? That was the honor of Lord Byron and of Mosby and it will be my honor and I will have this house for refuge. If there is anything wrong with Jack there is always this family and they will prevail on him and make things right. I will marry this house, she thought. She wondered where their room would be.

Upstairs, Jack blew out the kerosene lamp. His books were in darkness now. The moonlight and chill autumn air came in through the window. He closed the window and groped his way to the stairs carrying the briefcase in one hand and the rifle in the other. As he emerged on the second-floor hallway the clock was striking ten. The phone in the upstairs hallway was ringing and, believing that it might be Woolworth, he picked it up; only it wasn't Woolworth but Pat Roosevelt.

Phoebe was listening to the grandfather, who sat there drinking a dark lowball with a red cherry in it, his spectacles glinting in the firelight.

He is teasing me, she thought.

"I bet you go out with a lot of the university fellows," he said.

"No," she said.

"A pretty girl like you has got to go out with about a couple of dozen."

She shook her head and denied it.

"Well, you ought to," the old man said. "There are a lot of other fellows than Jack. A lot of better fellows, too."

"Richard," the old woman said. That was the grandfather's name. But the old man sipped on his drink and looked into the fire and did not answer her.

"He is just joshing," the old woman said.

Dot said, "You never can tell about Father."

"If I was you," the old man said, "I would take my time and look around."

"I don't have time to," Jack was telling Roosevelt for the third time. He was already late for the meeting with Woolworth.

"I insist," Pat said.

"How about midnight, then?" Jack said.

"No," Pat said. "Right now. I'd dislike having to come over there and slap your face in front of your family."

"Yeah," Jack said. "You would dislike it, all right."

"Right now," Pat said.

"Okay."

"In the parking lot at the side of the hotel."

"Okay."

Now Jack went out onto the second-story back porch and walked softly down the stairs. Across the alley, above the garden's brick wall, Woolworth's study window was dark. Jack went quietly around the side of the house and down the yard's hill to Second Street, opened the rumble seat, put the rifle and briefcase in there, and retraced the route he had come. Then descended into the living room.

"I have to step out for a few minutes," he said.

"Do you want me to go with you?" Phoebe asked. It occurred to her that he might be leaving and not coming back.

"It will just take a few minutes," Jack said.

"You stay here with me," the grandfather told Phoebe.

Jack drove to the hotel, went directly into the side lot, and parked there. Some of the cars in the lot were strung with orange and black banners. A lot of noise was coming from the hotel: radio music, laughter, and loud talk. Pat's taxicab was parked next to the side door. Pat was standing there in the shadows with the Doctor. The Doctor was wearing his blue and gold doorman's uniform and looked like a Chilean admiral. He was carrying a black leather case. Jack took off his jacket and walked over to them.

"I understand you are going to slap my face," he said.

"We have to go somewhere else," Pat said.

Jack hit him in the stomach, doubling him over, and hooked him hard to the temple, but Pat had hold of his arm now and Jack felt himself spun and tripped and

137

thrown violently to the ground and Pat was on top of him holding him and rubbing his face into the ground and Jack tried to move and couldn't and now remembered the part about the wrestling. He tried to free himself and the harder he tried the harder his face was rubbed in the ground.

"I said not here," Pat muttered in his ear.

"All right," Jack said. Pat let go and stood and Jack came up throwing a straight right and caught him in the mouth and Pat came in on him and behind him and grabbed him in a hammerlock.

"I'm going to teach you how to behave like a gentleman," Pat said. He was very strong and he bent Jack's head forward. "This is your last chance." He released him and Jack stood there looking at him. Blood was coming in a thin dark line from the corner of Pat's mouth.

"Show him," Pat said.

Doctor opened the case. The oiled dueling pistols gleamed dully in the hotel's light.

"I will let you go if you're willing to leave the young lady alone," Pat said.

"Where does he want to go?" Jack asked.

"Golf course," Doctor wheezed.

"You can get a second if you want to," Pat said. "I am just doing this to give you an even chance."

There was no one in the parking lot.

"You can examine the weapons if you want to," Pat said.

"Are they loaded?" Jack asked.

"Not yet."

"You almost broke my neck."

"I could have broken it if I wanted to. I could kill you with my bare hands if I wanted to."

"That's against the law," Jack said.

"There are a lot of other things that ought to be against the law, too," Pat said. "You can choose your weapon or you can leave that girl alone."

"Let me see the pistols," Jack said.

"Help yourself."

Jack stepped a little closer to Pat and lifted one of the pistols out of the box. It was surprisingly heavy. There was an inscription on the handle wrought in old lettering: *From Bernie.* Jack stood there hefting the pistol in his hand.

"I don't think I better do it," he said.

"It's up to you," Pat said.

"I had better not do it."

Just then Pat put his hand up to where the blood was coming from and Jack smashed him across the face with the pistol, breaking his nose. Pat came at him and Jack stepped aside and smashed him in the eye and Pat went down and Jack kicked him in the side of the head then leaped on top of him and smashed him in the jaw with the pistol and now Pat was not moving and there was much blood oozing from his nose.

Doctor got down clumsily on one knee, looking.

"You got to get him out of here," he said.

"I'll take him up to the hospital."

"Can't do that," Doctor said. "Both of us go to jail for fifteen or twenty years."

There were voices now out in front of the hotel.

"I already done forty years," Doctor said.

Jack ran over to the Model A and backed it up to where Roosevelt was.

"Put him in the back," Doctor said. There was a lot of blood flowing from Pat's nose, which had been smashed flat. One of his eyes was closed, too, and there was blood coming from that. Jack grabbed him by the back of the collar, lifted him, and pushed him slithering in his own blood across the car's fender and into the rumble seat, where Pat toppled over onto the floor. Now the talkers were coming around the corner and Jack closed the rumble seat.

"Is he dead?" Jack asked.

Doctor shrugged and merged away darkly into the shadows and now the talkers were there. They were young people Jack's own age and they were passing a silver flask around among them. They stopped and passed it to Jack and he took a long, scalding drink.

"That was some kind of game," a blond fellow said. He was the one whose father owned the coal mines.

"Yeah, it was pretty good," Jack said.

"I'd like for you to meet my fiancé, Miss Trice," the blond fellow said.

"How do you do?" Jack said.

"She is from the Pittsburgh Trices," the blond fellow said.

When Jack drove out of the parking lot the courthouse clock read ten forty-five. He went back to Second Street and parked out front again. There were more people in the living room now. There were his grandparents and his three sisters with their dates. His kid brother was just climbing up the stairs to bed.

"Let's play catch tomorrow," he called back.

"Sure," Jack said.

Phoebe was listening to his grandfather, who was speaking to her intensely about something. The young people were talking about the Sewanee game. His mother, as usual, was sitting plumply and smiling at the young people. She seemed always to approve of what they did. His father's chair was empty.

"We have to get going," Jack said.

Phoebe looked up at him, looked him in the eyes for the first time. She was beautiful.

"All right," she said. "I just have to step next door and get a few things."

"We ought to go now."

"Let this girl alone," her grandfather said. To Phoebe he said, "If I was you I wouldn't go with him any place. There are a lot of snakes in the grass."

"You mean there are a lot of fish in the sea," the grandmother put in.

"I mean what I said."

But Phoebe had gone. As Jack was about to follow her, he felt his grandmother's hand on his arm.

"Jack," she said.

"Yes, ma'm."

"I want you to be gentle, Jack."

"Yes, ma'm."

The old lady reached down and took his hand and held it. She had gotten to be very frail and not her lavender shawl or any shawl could hide that any more.

The mantel clock struck the hour. Jack went out front. It was very cold now, close to freezing, and the stiff wind whipped the leaves off the tall trees. They came in squadrons blackly sideways whizzing down the street. He went to the car. Something was dripping down from under the back. It was dripping steadily and there was already a pool of it on the street. He climbed the stairs again, opened the latticework door under the porch. He got out the hose, turned on the water, and went down the hill, unraveling it, to where the car was and sprayed the water under the car where the pool had gathered. As he was putting the hose away he saw his grandmother standing on the front porch.

"It's too cold out here for you," he said.

141

"I wish I could help you," she said.

"You have helped me," he said. "You have always helped me."

Phoebe was coming around the side of the house carrying a little paper suitcase with a sticker saying *New York City* on the side.

His grandmother stretched out her hand and there was money in it.

"I wish it was a million dollars," she said.

"No," Jack said. "I can't take it. I will make a million dollars, and I will get you everything you want."

"Ready," Phoebe said. She did not see the grandmother.

They went down to the car. As Jack was opening the passenger door for the girl, whose first name he did not remember, he saw his grandmother on the porch waving goodbye. Go back in and read it, he thought. Read it some more and I hope it makes you feel good. He wondered whether he would ever see her again and what denomination the bills had been. He was holding himself under control. Probably ones, he thought. He never gives her any more than that. I can sell the watch. If I get that far.

He drove up to Vinegar Hill and turned into the cobblestoned alley separating Marguerita's from the manger.

"There are some colored people in there," he said.

"I thought you wanted to go tonight," the girl said.

"I do. But you are going to have to wait in there for a little while."

"It suits me," she said. "I grew up around colored people."

He led her in the back door and down the hallway to Marguerita's office. As they were passing the back parlor he saw Woolworth sitting at the table, looking at his wrist watch. He wasn't wearing any little pink party hat, either.

"You're late," Marguerita said. Then she saw the girl.

"She has got to stay here for a few minutes," Jack said. "No."

"She has got to." He led Phoebe over to the bed, pushed some romance magazines aside, and made her sit down.

"You're in bad trouble," Marguerita said.

As he was leaving, Jack passed by the parlor again and this time Woolworth spotted him.

"Cabell!"

"I will be back in a minute," Jack said.

He went out in the alley where the car was hidden behind a shed. He opened the rumble seat, climbed in, and fished out Roosevelt from the floor, two hands clutched on his coat and lugging him like a sack of grain. He got him down slithering over the fender, lugged him into the manger, and heaved him up onto the long table there. George Gordon came in.

"What is it?" Gordon asked. Pat was still bleeding profusely from the shattered nose.

"Get the Doctor," Jack said.

"You got to move this man out of here," Gordon said.

"Get the Doctor," Jack said. "He and me are both going to jail if you don't. He has got to fix him."

Gordon came over to the table and looked down at Roosevelt. "How long has he been bleeding like this?" he asked.

"You had better get the Doctor," Jack said.

Gordon left.

Jack looked down at Pat. The good eye was open and the lips were moving, but no words were coming out.

"You are going to be all right," Jack said. "I'm going to look after you." There were leather ankle straps and he put them on Pat and cinched them. Now Pat lay there with his thighs spread like a Negress getting an abortion. There was a thick chest strap and Jack put that on and cinched it tight. Then he put on the wrist straps, with Pat trying to keep him from doing it and still trying to talk. Pat's face was very pale.

Jack went back to the car, got the rifle, and closed the rumble seat. There was blood on the rifle and he went over to the spigot, turned on the water, and washed it. The water was still warm from the summer but the alley was bitingly cold and the wind whipped down it. Through the window Jack could see Phoebe on the bed talking to Marguerita. They will get along all right, Jack thought. They will agree with each other. They have probably got the same philosophy. I never saw one of them that didn't.

He went inside and hid the rifle in the corner of the towel closet. And now entered the parlor, where Wool-worth sat with a cup of black coffee at his elbow and his arms in front of him on the yellow tablecloth.

Pat was trying to come to. He had never been knocked out before and it was hard to come to. He would be conscious for a little while and then he would fall back again into what was like sleep, then he would know it wasn't sleep and would be coming to and he was uneasy but wasn't wide awake enough to be frightened. He was in a hospital, he thought; he saw Jack standing there above him and tried to resist when Jack was strapping his wrists but then he fell asleep again. When he woke up he felt strangely weak and he was breathing with difficulty out of his mouth and he hawked and weakly spat some blood out of the corner of his mouth and then the breathing was easier and he was all the way awake and he was alone and knew that this was no hospital. Pat was frightened. It seemed he was in some sort of place that had once been a garage. He was alone for a long time and his head was buzzing and he tried to loose himself from the straps. His nose seemed to cover half his face and he could feel the warm trickle as something flowed steadily out of his nose and down his cheek.

He heard a sound like a soughing, and a wheezing he recognized as familiar, and Doctor hove in, limping sideways, the way he always walked, wearing the doorman's blue uniform.

"Thank God," Pat said.

The Doctor came over to the table and looked down at him. He took Pat's forehead in his hands and turned his head gently one way and another, looking at him. A second Negro, a taller, younger man with a cigarette dangling from the corner of his mouth, came in now and was closing the door.

"Thank God," Pat said.

Doctor didn't say anything.

The tall Negro was carrying a straw hat. "Is this yours?" he asked.

"Yes," Pat said. "Take these straps off, please."

"Go get that fool," Doctor told the tall one. George Gordon left.

"Please take the straps off," Pat said. "They're hurting my wrists."

"I will see if I can ease them for you," Doctor said. He let the straps out one notch, but they were still tight.

"You don't understand," Pat said. "I want them off."

"Where is she?" Woolworth asked Jack. They were sitting at the back parlor table across from one another with a cone of light from the pool table lamp shining down on the yellow tablecloth between them.

Jack just looked at him. In the past he had felt prompted to answer quickly when Woolworth spoke. But that was all gone out of him now and he sat there for a long minute looking at the man and thinking, I would like to put a bullet in that eye.

"She is up the road," Jack said.

"What road?"

Jack shook his head.

"I can have you thrown in jail right now," Woolworth said.

"Yes," Jack said. "But I will make bond."

"I doubt it," Woolworth said.

"Maybe if you had gone to law school you'd know better," Jack said. Woolworth was a big, hard man and Jack could see something in his face of what he must have looked like when he rode into Charlottesville at fifteen. He had come from someplace in Illinois and had got a job as a grease monkey down at the railroad yard.

An intense, strange feeling was coming over Jack. I want to kill him, he thought. I would rather kill him than have it work out. Woolworth's face across the yellow tablecloth turned suddenly ashen and Jack thought, He can read me. He has been able to read me all along and that is how he got my number. Well, let him read me now.

"What do you want?" Woolworth asked.

Jack had forgotten that he wanted anything. What he really wanted was to kill the man. He had not known this.

"What is it?" Woolworth said.

It was very hard to think of what it was. At last Jack heard himself say it.

"I want to finish school," he said. "I am a member of your family now, and I want to finish school." As he was

146

speaking the side door opened and the police chief walked in. His holster was unsnapped.

"What do you mean, you are a member of my family?" Woolworth asked.

Jack told him, only not the exact truth; said he and the London girl were already married.

"Like hell," Woolworth said.

"She is in there talking with your girlfriend right now."

"Where? Who?"

"Down the hall," Jack said.

Woolworth looked up at the police chief. "Go see," he said. The chief left. Woolworth took a sip of the black coffee. His hand was trembling.

"You think you're pretty smart, don't you?" he said.

The chief came back in the room. His uniform was like the Doctor's, only the blue was darker. Woolworth looked up at him and the chief nodded. "Get out of here," Woolworth said.

Then they were alone again.

"You can finish your law school," Woolworth said.

"I have got to," Jack said. "I have got to have a life." The killing urge was leaving him now and his heart was hammering rapidly with the violence of its passing.

"But the day you finish I want you out of this town."

"All right," Jack said. It really made very little difference where a man lived, he reflected, so long as he was awake when he was there and not running around to ancestors for advice.

"I don't like you," Woolworth said.

Jack stood up. "Well, I will be going," he said. He'd really known all along, but had not admitted, that other people were like himself, that some people did not like other people and that there was no special reason.

"Go on up and practice your law in Rappahannock County or whatever godforsaken place that is. But you are no family of mine."

"I had better finish the school," Jack said.

"Don't worry about that," Woolworth said. "I am not like you. I have got a word. I have bought and paid for it."

When Jack emerged into the hall, George Gordon was standing there waiting for him.

"Is he all right?" Jack asked.

"Come on," Gordon said.

Jack followed him. There were many students in the front parlor, laughing and talking and passing flasks around, and much traffic on the stairs. Marguerita liked girls who worked fast.

Jack and Gordon went across the alley to the manger. Gordon locked the door behind them. Pat Roosevelt was up on the table where Jack had left him, strapped by the ankles and wrists and with the thick strap around his chest. His face had been wiped clean of the black clots and red blood was still welling from his nose.

"Please tell them to take the straps off," Pat said. He was very pale.

"Take the straps off him," Jack said.

"I think you done drove a sliver of bone back in the brain," the Doctor said. He'd removed the doorman's coat and was wearing a black apron that came up to his chin. The apron was about the same color he was.

"Take the straps off and I will get him to the hospital," Jack said.

The Doctor shook his head.

"No," he said.

"For God's sake," Pat said. He was looking at Jack. "You are a white man. Make them take the straps off."

"Can you fix him?" Jack asked.

"I got to fix him," Doctor said.

Jack didn't like the tone of that and turned to go back for the rifle but Gordon was standing right behind him with the derringer pointed at his belly.

"What are you going to do?" Pat said.

Jack turned around and saw the razor in Doctor's hand. It was a long straight razor with a black bone handle and he flicked the gleaming blade out now.

"I am just going to let some blood out of your neck," Doctor said. He reached down and held Pat's head to one side like a barber does.

Pat was trying to squirm away.

"Please no," he said. "Please no."

"Take it easy," the Doctor said. "It ain't going to hurt. You ain't going to feel it." He was trying to steady the head.

"Don't," Jack said.

"It ain't going to hurt him," Doctor said.

Pat was squirming violently.

"Take it easy," Doctor said. "You got to learn to take it easy." His bulky figure was between Jack and Pat now and there was a quick slicing movement and the body's jerk and blood spurting up to the ceiling all at once and then the body was still.

The Doctor turned around. His face was covered with blood.

"I told him it wasn't going to hurt," he said.

Jack's knees were shaking violently and it was difficult to stand. He looked down at the straw-strewn dirt floor and then up at the Doctor, who was mopping the blood from his face with a bandanna. Gordon slipped the derringer back into his pocket. It was quiet.

"Where is the saw?" Doctor asked.

"Over on the shelf," Gordon said.

"I mean the hacksaw."

"It's there, too."

"What about the buckets?" Doctor asked.

"I'll go get them," Gordon said.

"You had better get some towels or something else to put over the top of them when we haul him out," Doctor said.

Then Gordon was gone.

"Are you going to kill me?" Jack asked. He was still dizzy and did not look at the thing on the table.

"Ain't nobody going to kill you," the Doctor said. "You going to have a long life. You and me is in this good long life together."

"I won't tell," Jack said.

"We know you ain't going to tell," Doctor said. He had wiped most of the blood off now. "Because you was the one that done it."

It was very difficult to drive the car. Jack was trembling violently. The road from Charlottesville arrowed toward Maryland and was absolutely straight the way Mr. Jefferson had planned it. A fox went scurrying across the road in the glare of the headlamps. It was hard to stay on the road because of the trembling. Phoebe was riding beside him in the passenger seat. She was wearing a sweater.

"I liked Mrs. Gordon," she said.

They were headed for Buckeystown, Maryland, just over the state line, where there was no waiting period. Jack had been drinking ever since they'd left Charlottesville, straight whiskey out of the bottle, and it had done nothing for him.

So this is what it means to be a man, Jack thought. Well, I have got to forget what happened. I have got to forget what I have seen and remember what I know. What her father said is so about that word he could not pronounce and he is crazy because he knows it but I am going to have to know it and not be crazy; although not tonight. Jack had not slept for three days now and had seen small yellow devils lurking in the corners of the car and was thinking to himself, they are probably real, all right, but when I have slept and more time has passed I will not see them any more and I will believe they are not real. They slipped out of radios when you snapped the dials and sometimes they went back and sometimes didn't. But he would forget all the things he knew for sure now and could not bear. For instance, he was sure that the amber moon pulled all the cars on all the highways, or pushed them, and that the moon as well controlled the mechanical motions of his body. But I will forget that when I have slept, he thought. He would be glad to sleep. He would be glad to have a place to sleep and would trade the watch and the ring both for that. Because you could always get another watch or another ring, or do without them. But fast time ran here out in the world that was no longer totally green and one needed to sleep if one was to live out here; one needed to forget what one had seen and remember only what it meant.

They passed under the Cabell oak tree in Rappahannock some time after midnight and he asked her if she wanted to stop for anything. She had said something about getting her father's permission.

"Let's wait and see if there are any lights on," she said. But there weren't and they drove on.

Old Man Jim was sitting in the front yard with his hands jammed down into the mackinaw pockets. There had not been a car in more than an hour but he heard this one coming and saw the smudge of light as it passed, carrying his daughter away to the dreams she'd always had of a firm alliance with honor. Old Man Jim could not see the stars, although by now the cold wind had blown the clouds away and it was a clear night. But he could hear the airplanes when they came over. He could hear them from a long way off. And he could hear a car, too, as it approached, and long after it had passed.

They had radios in the cars now, he'd heard, and he wondered if the people in that car were listening to the radio, and what they would hear. He was getting sleepy now and soon would go inside to his own room. Rappahannock was dark. The car was gone and the road was quiet.